Brave

Man

Dead

Hannah Blank

Brave

Man

Dead

Hightrees Books
Imprint of Prism Corporation
New York

Published by Hightrees Books,
         an Imprint of Prism Corporation
         P.O.Box 20775, Cherokee Station
         New York, New York 10021-0075

Library of Congress Catalog Card Number 00-110265

Blank, Hannah
Brave Man Dead /
Hannah Blank

p.cm.

ISBN 0-9652778-3-6

Printed in the United States of America

10 9 8 7 6 5 4 3 2 1

"It is not righteousness to outrage

a brave man dead,

not even though you hate him. "

--Sophocles' *Ajax*

HISTORICAL NOTE

After the separate peace France made with Hitler in 1940, more than half of France was occupied by the Germans. Paris was included in this portion. The unoccupied portion was administered by the so-called Vichy government, where living conditions for the French were no better.

World War II ended in Europe in 1944, but a decade later France, Germany and other European countries still needed assistance in rebuilding. The United States through the Marshall Plan provided enormous financial assistance for reconstructing Western European countries, not just our allies but countries such as France which rolled over for the Nazis within a month of the German invasion of France, and Germany, which of course was on the other side in the war. Japan was also greatly aided both economically and politically. Besides economic aid in reconstruction, we assisted Germany and Japan in establishing democratic systems. In the 1950's, the time period of this novel, there were many U.S. Army bases and offices, and other U.S. governmental agencies, engaged in administering these vast programs.

1

Ever since his April wedding in America, and his return to his desk at the Paris *Police Judiciare*, Dantan's malaise had been growing.

He should have been a happy man. Where he had previously served in a tedious post only as interpreter, after the *Rue des Ecoles* case* he had been promoted to Inspector. He was well-regarded by his chief and affectionately accepted by his fellow inspectors (one of whom, a true friend indeed, had gotten him into the P.J. after his discharge from the army).

Three months ago he had married an adorable, amusing, sexy young lady from a rich family.

But American.... And Jewish.... Was that the cause of his unease? With a few exceptions he and his friends tended to scorn Americans. And although

A MURDER OF CONVENIENCE [1999; Hightrees Books]

Dantan himself felt no antisemitism -- he had been transported as a child from wartime France to England, where he was raised with a pack of refugee children, mostly Jewish -- he knew that antisemitism was prevalent among his acquaintances and that at best, the Jew in France was looked upon as "different." But if he had survived the wounds and horrors of the war in Indochina he could hold his own with rich American Jewish in-laws!

No, his malaise could not be explained that way.

He thought he knew what it was. He was worried whether he could repeat the success he had had in the *Rue des Ecoles* case. As a mere interpreter, there had been no pressure on him then. He had not been expected to solve anything. That he was the one to solve the case had been a happy surprise for all, not least of all himself. Now he was expected to perform such feats; it was his job.

It had been an unusually happy time for him. Before he had become involved with the case at *Rue des Ecoles* he had cared about little. His work as an interpreter was tiresome, although of course he was glad to have a job. And he was going through the motions of sex with a little *amie* he liked but knew he would not miss should they separate.

Then he was sent to a *pension* on *Rue des Ecoles* to interpret for the P. J. inspectors as they interrogated the five resident American students who lived in the building where a French woman had been found murdered.

One of the Americans, Judy Kugel, was a bubbly delightful young woman, *tres* sexy, liberal and enthusiastic with her favors. They began a very enjoyable affair. Slim and fit, Dantan was a dark and intelligent-looking young man of twenty-seven, and they enjoyed each other very much. Judy wanted to get married. Marriage seemed out of his reach at that time, as he had only his modest salary. But Judy's rich father, despite his misgivings at having a foreign son-in-law, offered the pair a very generous dowry. The happiness of his daughter was paramount. So, after Dantan's promotion, he and Judy became engaged, then joined in matrimony as soon as Judy's mother could orchestrate an extravant lavish wedding in Great Neck, New York.

In the six months since his promotion early in 1954, there had been no major crimes to solve. He had only minor achievements because there had been only minor challenges; he had assisted, in a small way, in cracking an Algerian terrorist ring; he had been the liaison between NATO and assorted governmental bureaus and secretariats on the protection of royalty during a week-long visit; he had been instrumental in retrieving stolen passports and jewelry (though not the cash) from a burglary at the sumptuous apartment in Passy rented by an American official.

The rest of his time had been spent on paperwork, meetings, getting better acquainted with the specialists such as the forensic technicians and photographers, his own study of files and *dossiers* to learn from past cases and procedures, assisting in the interrogation of not-very-important English-speaking witnesses, and drinking with his best friend Jean-Jacques Pilieu and the other inspectors.

Even Bastille Day had come and gone with only the most minor of disturbances. There had been only one fatality, and that was not the result of violence. A silly youth had painted his entire nude body, including his penis, with gold paint for the parade, and had died of asphyxiation.

Dantan was itching for a real murder case, and of course, he urgently wanted to be the one to solve it.

It didn't help his mood that their apartment had been in disorder since they returned from their wedding three months before. Dantan was a meticulous individual. He disliked disorder, whether it was his person, his desk, or his home, and he was now living in a place that was in extreme disorder and had been for three months, with the end not yet in sight.

He would have preferred that they rent a modest place in an inexpensive neighborhood, something they could afford on his inspector's salary. But Judy's parents, already upset that their baby girl was settling down in a foreign land with a foreign man and one with no real money, were determined to provide the couple with as many of the comforts of the United States in general, and Great Neck, Long Island, New York in particular, as they could.

Hence, Mr Kugel's purchase of a large, once-elegant, but now dilapidated apartment near the Luxembourg Gardens, Judy's preferred location. Foreign nationals were not permitted to own French real estate, so Mr Kugel had made the purchase in Dantan's name. He had made sure that Dantan understood what a gesture of trust this was. Dantan knew that he himself was a man who could be trusted, and he welcomed his father-in-law's trust, but he would have preferred that he and Judy live solely on his salary. Judy, however, was delighted that her father was buying them the apartment, and Mr Kugel himself was only too happy to do it.

Mr Kugel was a decisive, even aggressive, businessman and difficult to resist.

When Dantan and Judy became engaged back in late January, her parents had flown to Paris for the occasion. Mister Kugel gave a dinner for eight people at Maxim's to celebrate the engagement and Dantan's promotion resulting from Dantan's successful solution of the *Rue des Ecoles* case.

Soon after the dinner, or rather, after the days it took him and his wife to recover from the overly-rich meal and an unaccustomed amount of wine, Mr Kugel flew back to the States to tend to his business, while Judy and her mother, after a week-long shopping spree on the *Faubourg Saint Honoré*, sailed home on the *Normandie* to prepare for the wedding. Dantan was not happy to be separated from Judy for so long, but Mrs Kugel was also forceful in her own way. She was in firm control of the wedding preparations, the menu, the flowers, the guest-list, the bridal gown, the selection of bridesmaids, the supervision of their gowns.... She needed Judy in Great Neck for multiple bridal-gown fittings, and Judy wanted to be there to do battle with her mother over the choice of bridesmaids. Mrs Kugel favored the daughters of her own friends; Judy disliked some of them and wanted her own friends.

For several weeks, Judy and Dantan wrote passionate letters to each other, but it wasn't the same as being together.

Then one day in March, Dantan was startled at his new inspector's desk by the pale youth whose job was to fetch and deliver coffees and sandwiches and to bring visitors up. The errand-boy informed Dantan that there was a transatlantic telephone call for him in the Chief Inspector's office. (The inspectors had no phones of their own but shared one in the general workroom where the clerks and translators toiled.) He hurried to his boss's office, perturbed at the thought that his fiancee was intruding upon his professional hours, and disturbing his boss besides. But Chief Inspector Goulette took this intrusion with good humor, and left the new inspector to have privacy with his call.

Dantan was about to berate Judy for her unac-
ceptable breach of protocol, when he heard, not
Judy's voice being put through by the operator, but
his future father-in-law's. "You'll forgive me for calling you at work," Mr Kugel grumbled, not sound-
ing at all repentant, "but how else was I to call you?
You people must start getting telephones installed
over there! Anyway, to get to the point. Alphonse, I
looked around at living conditions in Paris before I
left and I assess the chances of you two finding anything civilized, other than a furnished sub-rental
from an American, are nil. So I've decided to buy
you two an apartment and fix it up properly. I'm
coming to Paris next week, and in the meantime, I
want you to find at least three or four properties for
me to look at. I'll buy the best one and put it in your
name. I know Americans can't own real estate in
France. Another reason your economy is still in the
dumps, your government won't allow foreign investment, only handouts. But that's another story.
Alphonse, get those places lined up and telegraph
me as soon as you've done so. I can fly right over
and settle the matter. No time to lose, as it takes you
Frogs forever and a day to get anything done and I
would like my baby to have a bathtub and a telephone by the time she's married and moved over
there. *D'accord?*"

D'accord, Dantan had noticed, was the only
French word his future father-in-law had learned,

probably because he always expected everyone to agree with him.

"*D'accord, Monsieur* Kugel," Dantan replied, although he had no idea at that moment how to set about finding apartments for sale, other than checking the newspaper classifieds.

After apologizing to Chief Inspector Goulette, and giving him a brief explanation of the call, Dantan returned to his desk to muddle over trivial paperwork while most of his attention was focussed on Mr Kugel's request – or rather, command.

At noon, Dantan and Jean-Jacques went for a meal to a neighborhood brasserie, where Dantan told his friend about Mr Kugel's telephone call. Jean-Jacques was elated for his friend, pointing out the degree of trust Dantan's future father-in-law was placing in him, not only by putting the apartment in Dantan's name, but doing so before the wedding.

Pilieu was also of practical assistance. His father had been acquainted with an *administrateur provisoire* under the Vichy regime, the very sort of person to know the whereabouts of good properties for sale.

The position of *administrateur provisoire* had been created under a German ordinance in 1940. It provided for an administrator who would take over Jewish property and "aryanize" it, since the Jews who owned it had been deported to death camps or had, if they were lucky, fled with their lives.

M. Gervaise had been an a.p. for many Jewish properties, commercial as well as residential. Dantan did not know, nor did he want to know, how it was that these four apartments should have remained in the possession of the a.p. almost a decade after the end of the war. But if *M.* Gervaise could establish legal ownership, something for Mr Kugel and his lawyer to determine, not Dantan, then perhaps it was as well that one of the properties, at least, should pass into the hands of a Jew once more.

It took only a few days to meet Pilieu's *administrateur provisoire* acquaintance, and line up four apartments for Mr Kugel to view. *M.* Gervaise was a distinguished looking man about sixty, dressed in a dark English-cut suit, expensive-looking, highly shined black shoes, and an air of confidence which implied a contempt for anyone who couldn't match his sartorial elegance. He looked the same when he attended the meeting with the Kugels, father, mother, daughter, who flew over as soon as Dantan informed them there was something to see. He proposed *déjeuner* first.

Dantan had had to take a day off without pay in order to show the Kugels the four apartments he had found for their consideration. He did not want to spend time over a leisurely meal first.

Mr Kugel seemed to appreciate Dantan's impatience immensely. His future son-in-law appeared to be acquiring the American sense of urgency, and the willingness to forgo a rich leisurely meal in order to get on with business. This boded well for his future success amid a working population which, as far as Mr Kugel could determine, did as little as possible and devoted more interest and attention to their *dejeuners* than to their work.

Dantan picked up the Kugels at their hotel in the *Palais Royale.* He exchanged only a few passionate kisses with Judy, who was bubbling with excitement. She was still plump, but seemed to have lost a few kilos.

They met *M.* Gervaise at the building on *Rue de Vaugirard,* directly beside the Luxembourg Gardens.

M. Gervaise was waiting for them in the concierge's loge. Mr Kugel, who was short and round, looked approvingly at the distinguished, expensively tailored French attorney. Dantan performed the introductions, and M. Gervaise shook hands all around. The five of them then proceeded up a wide and winding oak staircase to the third floor, to the first of the apartments they were to see. They walked through its ample, elegant but decaying rooms in silence, Judy because she was afraid of disrupting her father's thought-processes, Mrs Kugel because she was out of breath from the stairs, and Mr Kugel because he had no intention of giving *Monsieur* Gervaise a hint of what he was thinking.

Then it was on to the next building and apartment on *M.* Gervaise's list, on the *Rue des Medicis,* where they climbed four flights of stairs. Then the next and the next. All were in the vicinity of the Luxembourg Gardens, but although the distances were not great between them, there were many, many steps up and and many, many steps down and by the fourth apartment, plump Mrs Kugel was more than winded. She was near collapse. And there was no place for her to sit down. None of the apartments had contained furniture. It was therefore not surprising that she was not entusiastic about any of the apartments she had seen.

In fact, Mrs Kugel was horrified at all four. She had envisioned a Hollywood-movie setting for her precious little girl. She knew almost nothing of the realities of contemporary Parisian life just nine years after the end of World War II. Each time she and her husband had visited the city they had stayed in a double suite at the *Palais Royale*. They took taxis; ate at Maxim's. The rooms she had just seen were dingy and barren, permeated by musty odors, and with no glistening kitchen appliances, no bathrooms at all.

All of the apartments were filthy, and in need of repairs and painting. And in deference to the sensibilities of his American bride, they also needed installation of modern bathroom fixtures. But they were all in good locations near the Luxembourg Gardens, just as his darling Judy had required.

The rooms were amply and elegantly proportioned. To Dantan, who knew nothing about real estate, the purchase prices did seem reasonable.

And they were vacant. A major benefit, since removing a tenant who had a lease was all but impossible. In fact, there were apartment-seekers who regularly read the obituaries so as to track down the residences which might have become empty. Occasionally, one saw in the classifieds a poignant advertisement placed by an elderly person, offering her apartment for sale, to be paid in full at once, with possession to be taken upon the owner's death.

All four of the apartments they viewed with *M.* Gervaise were owned by *M.* Gervaise, their legitimate owners no doubt long since dead.

In the *Rue des Ecoles* case, Dantan had encountered such an apartment, plundered by Frenchmen after the Jewish owners had been deported.

Mr Kugel did not view the apartments in the same light as his wife did. He knew that with sufficient expenditures any of them could be renovated to his daughter's liking and to American standards of plumbing. He was prepared to spend whatever it took to do so, especially when he heard how low the purchase prices were.

After Mr Kugel assured *Monsieur* Gervaise he would be in touch very very soon, and the latter had departed, Dantan and the Kugels adjourned to a nearby *café*, where they ordered *croque-monsieurs*, beer for the men, mineral water for the ladies. Now out of *M.* Gervaise's hearing. Mr Kugel pronounced the prices so ludicrously low that he was prepared to buy all four of them as an investment.

Paris, he announced, would eventually get out of the dumps. It was a place that stirred everyone's imagination. One of these days, when the French fixed up some decent hotels, and installed some modern bathrooms instead of those silly *bidets,* and cleaned the streets, which were filthy, tourists would come in droves. This city was so revered world-wide that when the Germans were on their triumphal march into Paris, a high-ranking German officer risked his neck by countermanding Hitler's order to destroy "The City of Lights."

As he spoke more and more eloquently, Mr Kugel became quite enthusiastic on investing in Paris, forgetting that his original intention had been merely to provide decent living conditions for his precious daughter.

Dantan had to remind his future father-in-law that on a policeman's salary he could not be expected to be able to afford four apartments. Even one, of such generous proportions, was questionable. And since to comply with French law, the property would have to be in the name of a Frenchman, it would look highly suspicious if "Dantan" suddenly bought more than one place.

Mr Kugel waved away this objection. A way would be found. After all, the French expected a new bride to bring a *dot*, or dowry, didn't they? These apartments could be Judy's *dot*. He would renovate all the apartments, not just the one the young marrieds would occupy, then furnish them and rent them at exorbitant rents to Americans, who, working for various parts of the U.S. government, were rolling in dough.

Judy had not said one single word since the trek from apartment to apartment had begun; an unnatural state for her, and clearly attributable to her terror that her father would change his mind!

Mr Kugel weighed the relative advantages of each place aloud, but did not consult his wife or his daughter -- and certainly not his prospective son-in-law – on which apartment to select for the couple and therefore the first to be renovated. Finally, he settled upon the second one they had seen on the *Rue des Medicis*. It had four large bedrooms, two huge salons separated by glass doors, a huge but old-fashioned kitchen, a large pantry, a large storeroom off the foyer, which Mr Kugel pointed out could be converted into a splendid bathroom, and an ample foyer. Its principal salon, one of whose large windows was actually a door to a small balcony, overlooked the Luxembourg Gardens.

As soon as he announced his choice, Judy bounded out of her wicker chair, knocking it to the *café* floor, and hugged and kissed her daddy over and over.

Mr Kugel would first talk to his attorney in New York, and get a recommendation for a French attorney in Paris, and take it from there. He gave Dantan his office phone number and requested that Dantan call him daily, collect, at seven in the morning, Paris time, and he would be sure to be there for the call before going out to lunch. This was to give Alphonse instructions or information for the day.

Dantan expected to be somewhat embarassed when the other inspectors learned the details of his new place. But not because the father-in-law was paying for it. That was an expected part of a marriage settlement. It was because he felt that they would suspect him of marrying Judy Kugel for her family's money, when in fact, although the money did no harm, he truly was in love with his darling sweetheart.

Mr Kugel went back to his hotel to telephone *Monsieur* Gervaise of his decision, to telephone his attorney in Great Neck, and get the legal paperwork going. Mrs Kugel went off shopping, and Judy and Dantan retired to his little room to make love. A completely satisfying day for everyone.

The next morning, back at his desk, studiously examining the papers that had piled up in absence, Dantan was very quiet on the subject of the Kugels' visit, the momentous purchase to be made in his name, and the wedding in general. His only remarks on the subject were to murmur to Pilieu that the date had been set for the eighteenth of April, so he had better start making his arrangements with the chief inspector for the necessary days off to make the flight and return trip. (Mister Kugel was going to pay all Pilieu's travel expenses as Dantan wanted him as best man and Jean-Jacques could not have afforded to go to America otherwise.) Pilieu, who retained a certain amount of religious involvement, happened to know that that the eighteenth of April was Easter Sunday. He would be flying in on Good Friday. He was uncomfortable with this. But he did end his internal dilemma by agreeing to participate by leaving on Maundy Thursday instead.

After completing the paperwork to buy the apartment, Mr Kugel had proceeded to order all sorts of improvements for it: not one, but two American bathrooms resplendent with big tubs, enclosed showers, toilets, as well as the obligatory *bidet;* a gleaming American kitchen with a real refrigerator, among other rare appliances; and improved wiring so that they could run the refrigerator and eventually install rare air-conditioning; and a telephone. All the appliances and plumbing equipment would have to be shipped from the United States, at a time and cost Mr Kugel had chosen to overlook, in order to have a plan that would satisfy his baby girl, and something to look forward to during the long months when it would seem as if nothing was happening.

When Dantan and his bride returned from the States in April, the installation of all of these wonders was still in progress. He and Judy had to live amid chipped paint and falling plaster, construction materials, holes in the walls.... He would have liked to move back to his modest little hotel room where he and Judy had had some delightful moments before their marriage. But Judy (under the influence of her father, no doubt) insisted that they stay in the apartment to be close to the work and make sure it was going forth on schedule. As if anyone could get a French workman to do anything unless he wanted to do it!

Mercifully, two of the rooms had been largely completed and painted by the time the couple moved in. These were the "study" Judy had insisted on creating for him from a section of the large salon, and their bedroom. At least these two rooms were in relatively good order.

And the telephone had finally been installed in the still unfinished salon, thanks to Mr Kugel's incessant attempts to drive everyone at the telephone company crazy, and to pay them repeated bribes. This was his wife's lifeline to their daughter and as such, essential. The Kugels were spending hundreds of thousands of francs on the almost daily transatlantic phone calls to Judy. Jean-Jacques Pilieu had suggested to Dantan that perhaps the Kugels were trying to lure Judy back to them in the States, but

Dantan saw no evidence of that. Judy was not good at dissembling, and he would have suspected something if there had been anything to suspect.

Much of this was passing through his mind when the errand-boy summoned him to a telephone early Monday morning July 19th.

2

Miri Winter didn't particularly like her job. She thought of herself as an artist, but she worked as a clerk-typist at FOUSAP, the U.S. Army finance office in Paris. There was almost nothing to do. And the officers and civilians were all philistines, although to be absolutely fair, some of them were nice people.

There was Private Seymour Levin, of course, who had gotten her the job in the first place, and was very special in her life. But he was not always around. Actually that was probably a good thing. His friendly bear-hugs and almost incessant snuggling, while pleasant, also stirred some unidentifiable anxiety in her.

Seymour was tall and large, bearlike, with dark hair and deep brown eyes. And his ears stuck out. They had met the previous fall when he was still stationed in Germany, at Garmisch, and had come to Paris on a three-day pass. His mother had arranged for him to look up Judy Kugel, the daughter of a friend. Judy and Miri were then fellow *pensionnaires* at the *pension* Fleuris, while Miri was still an art student at the *Ecole des Beaux Arts*, and Judy was fooling around at the Sorbonne in a course for foreigners.

Judy brought Miri to the meeting she had set up at a *café* with Seymour Levin. That way he would have a harder time asking her for a date and in case she didn't like him she could tell her mother that "nothing had happened."

As it turned out, Judy thought he was nice enough, but Seymour made it clear immediately that he was attracted to Miri, her curves and her dark sultry looks, and her lack of consciousness of them. He found her solemn intellectuality amusing.

After his return to his base in Germany, he began writing to Miri frequently. He wrote on a high intellectual plane, which she liked, about serious books and serious music, that sort of thing, and he even started teaching her by mail how to play chess.

It was after he was transferred in January to the FOUSAP office in Paris, and became persistently amorous, that Miri became nervous. But she did like him, and did spend some nights with him at his apartment near *Notre Dame*. (If you stood up in the bathtub, you could see the cathedral.) The apartment had been furnished by the French owner, expressly to rent to Americans, but the previous tenant, also an American soldier, had replaced the French bed with one he had specially ordered from the States, a gigantic double bed, longer and wider than you could get in France.

Even after Seymour was transferred to Paris, he still made trips back and forth to Garmisch. When he was in the Paris office he had a desk in the basement machine-room, along with teams of machine-operators and the machine-room manager, Victor Logan, a career civilian. Seymour also had his own desk in the upstairs room shared with Private Dennis Bernardi, Private Peter Parnes, and Sergeant Carr Southwood. Seymour's enthusiasm for his work bored her, and she didn't pay much attention when he talked about it. Others, including Kitty Hill, secretary to Colonel Robert Ritchie in charge of FOUSAP, and his aide, Lieutenant John Morgan, sometimes also speculated on how a mere private could move back and forth so much. But even when they asked him, they learned nothing worth entering into the gossip pool.

Private Dennis Bernardi was a huge hulk of a guy with a big heart; he made people of laugh. He worked with the archives, stacks and stacks of old data printouts and filing-cabinets full of old official correspondence, the so-called "endorsements," which were memos written back and forth on the same pieces of paper, to economize. Miri thought it was funny that the Army was so thrifty, even stingy, with paper, when it wasted so much money on luxurious extras for the civilian employes, like paying a "hardship" allowance because they were living away from home (as if it was a hardship to live in Paris!) and paying to ship their cars all the way from the States.

Dennis sometimes went to lunch with Seymour at a nearby brasserie. Sometimes Seymour would ask Miri along.

When he tried to talk about the work he was doing, working with punch-cards and printouts, Seymour was boring, but the rest of the time he was interesting.

Dennis, on the other hand, was just plain boring. He was crazy about cars, especially large gaudy American cars. Every time Miri happened to walk with him through the front courtyard, which served as FOUSAP's parking lot, Dennis would point out the year and make of every American car parked there. And he knew who owned each one. Miri was embarassed at the vulgar ostentation of Americans driving around Paris in these brightly colored monsters when the French, who paid twice as much for gas but earned much less money, usually drove very small cars, if they could afford cars at all. And most of their cars were black.

Besides a pointless fascination with garish cars, Private Bernardi harbored a so-far unrequited passion for the skinny little young woman, Jackie Harris, who was the civilian manager of the archives and owned a red one-ton Mercury truck. He called her an "adorable grease monkey." She did look a bit like a monkey, as well as earning the epithet because she could take apart any engine, fix anything on a car, jack one up, change a tire, anything a real mechanic could do and perhaps more. Men would come to her for advice about their cars. Dennis over and over said that she was "unbelievably cute, with unbelievable energy."

Miri was not impressed. She thought Jackie looked like a bird of prey.

Miri liked her own boss, Charlie Nugent, an older man whose glasses were always slipping down his nose. Charlie loved gossip and would bring in home-baked brownies every Monday morning to make sure everyone in the office stopped by, hopefully with some new tidbit.

But the main thing Miri liked about her job was her salary. She was making what for her was a lot of money, more than half of which she was saving to be able to spend a year in Spain, painting. She had heard from art students at the *Beaux Arts* who had been to Spain that you could get a little whitewashed stone house on one of the Balearic Islands and live on a dollar a day. No one she met, however, had done much painting while they were there. They were having too good a time sitting in the *café* by

the docks, swigging Manzanilla or cognac for pen-
nies a glass, and gossiping with the English and
Swedes who had discovered the island and the
Manzanilla and the cognac too.

And she enjoyed her trip to the office in the
morning. She treated herself to *carnets* (ticket-books),
for First Class and always got a seat to herself. She
would sit there sketching other passengers after she
had made her transfer at Bastille. Then came a pleasant walk alongside a low wrought-iron fence bound-
ing a green park with tall trees.

Across the street from the park for a number of
blocks one stone mansion followed another on the
Rue Dante. Some were merely huge, others palatial.
The Finance Office of the U.S. Army, where she
was the second-lowliest person, a clerk-typist, was
one of the palatial ones. Ornate stone carvings
adorned its facade, and the wide flight of five steps
up to the ponderous carved door, was flanked by
Greco-Roman columns. The four-story mansion was
set well back from the street and wrapped around a
large cobblestone courtyard. Charlie had told her
he had heard that the Army had paid a lavish premium to the owner to get this particular mansion
because of its extra-large courtyard. They needed a
lot of parking for the Americans' cars.

By the time the work day began at eight-thirty,
the courtyard was filled. Thanks to Private Bernardi's
incessant instruction, Miri knew one monstrosity

from the other: a 1949 chartreuse Packard belonging to Tony Alotta, the portly supervisor of printing, who dashed off to the races as often as he could with his chubby girlfriend Harriet Barlow, supervisor of keypunching; a 1951 turquoise Packard, in which Terk Porter, one of the brawny luggers of boxes, made his daily liquor runs to the PX; Colonel Ritchie's discreet black 1952 Oldsmobile; a 1950 medium-brown Dodge driven by Vic Logan, the manager of the machine-room; a 1953 maroon Buick belonging to Mister Jayes; a 1953 green Chevrolet sedan, driven by Private Peter Parnes. He couldn't have afforded to buy a new car on his GI salary; the car had actually been bought by his roommate, Charlie Nugent. There was the 1952 dark blue Buick belonging to Carolene Mayce, the keypunching supervisor and a 1953 baby blue Cadillac belonging to Sergeant Carr Southwood. Southwood could afford a big new car even though he was just a sergeant because his family was rich. Kitty Hill said everyone wondered why he was stuck here in a finance office when his father could probably have gotten some congressman to get him a better assignment, but she happened to know Southwood had peculiar tastes. Paris was a good place for all that.

These vehicles dwarfed the one little black Peugeot owned by the sharp-faced overseer of the files, Jackie Harris. She used this car most of the time and she only drove her truck when she was going to take off after work for Germany, where she foraged for antiques. She was collecting Biedermeier, a ponderous sort of furniture she was planning to sell back in the States. Marjory Young, Vic Logan's secretary, had seen Jackie's collection and said it was hideous.

Lieutenant Morgan didn't drive because of his artificial leg. He took taxis.

Miri was continually horrified at and embarassed by the crass display of American money and bad taste which must make the French hate them even more. One of these days she would work herself up to do an intensely satiric painting of the courtyard full of the garish cars; that is, if she could contain her revulsion long enough.

Even the garden in the backyard, to the impotent dismay of neighbors on either side, had been paved over for more parking. On the days when Jackie brought in her big red truck she parked it in the back. The backyard also accommodated the bicycles, Velo-Solexes and Vespas belonging to the French members of the staff. Miri had once considered getting a Vespa, but didn't like the idea of riding it in the rain. She settled for a Velo-Solex, a bike.

Miri's little office adjoined Charlie's; the door between was usually left open. Charlie was the second-highest civilian in FOUSAP. The first-highest was Craig Jayes, whose big office was on the other side of Charlie's. These offices were all located on the so-called first floor, named in the French way;

that is, one flight up the wide winding staircase from the ground floor, where the grand marbled entryway was. Also on the "first" floor, across the hall from Jayes, Nugent and Miri, were the military heads, each in their own office, Colonel Ritchie, Lieutenant Morgan, and their secretary Kitty Hill.

Miri usually came in earlier than the official starting-time. That way she avoided stern glances from Lieutenant Morgan, a stocky sandy-haired man of medium height who walked with a slight limp. He had lost his leg at the battle of Anzio. Every morning he would stand at the bottom of the wide spiral staircase on the ground floor taking note of each person who came in. Anyone entering past eight-thirty would receive a severe reprimand.

Miri had once received one of those talking-to's and quickly resolved to arrive early enough to prevent it from happening again. It didn't matter that you might not have any work to do; you still had to get there on time to do nothing. The lieutenant also had a habit of dropping in unannounced at any one of the offices. But oddly, he didn't seem to mind if you had no work, as long as you were quiet and decorous, and were not conspiring on the phone with foreigners. He had found Miri sketching at her desk a few times, and even mumbled something complimentary.

It was a Monday, the morning of July 19th. Miri approached FOUSAP's stone mansion, its large

American flag hanging limply for lack of a breeze, on its tall flagpole. Charlie had told Miri that when the office was first opened and the flagpole installed and the flag raised, it had almost caused a diplomatic incident. Those French elite who had managed to retain ownership of their mansions did not want this blatant symbol of American imperialism marring a pristine scene on a French street of the upper-class.

But in the end, the American officers, stubbornly chauvinistic, prevailed. Their presence there, after all, was explained by the fact that America had been keeping France -- in fact all the European countries, including its recent enemies -- afloat financially since the war had ended.

The French owners of neighboring residences were monetarily compensated for their eventual concurrence that the American flag might remain. It quieted them, but it did not mollify them. They still hated the Americans and would have liked nothing better than to see them gone, leaving only their money behind them.

As yet, there were no cars in the courtyard.

Miri was surprised to see Kitty Hill, the plump curly-haired freckled flit who worked for the colonel and the lieutenant, standing by the front oak door, looking very upset. As Miri mounted the five stone steps to the entrance, Kitty stretched out her thick freckled arm, the pink ruffles on her short sleeve trembling, to bar the door.

"You can't go in there yet." Her voice was higher-pitched than usual; in fact she sounded hysterical. Miri had never seen her like this, not even when one of the French girls, coming to work on her bicycle, had been struck from behind by an auto and Kitty, much moved by her recital, in a heavy French accent, of the gory facts, had had to fill out an assortment of reports.

Kitty was always floating around gossiping, and in the mornings before the official workday had begun, Miri sometimes spotted her in the colonel's office perusing his files and humming to herself.

"Why not?"

When Kitty did not reply, Miri shoved her way past the other girl into the marble foyer. And she saw what had rattled Kitty. Unmoving, sprawled at the foot of the wide winding staircase was Lieutenant Morgan. His head was covered in blood, and there were pools of blood on the marble staircase.

"Have you called an ambulance?"

"He's dead," Kitty sobbed.

Miri, suddenly breathless and frightened, demanded to know if Kitty had called the police.

"I'm waiting for Colonel Ritchie," Kitty sobbed.

"What?"

"He'll know what to do."

Miri was sure she knew what to do, and it wasn't to wait for the colonel.

She dashed up the back stairs, formerly a servants' staircase, now used for carrying files and supplies up and down, and entered Mister Jayes' office on the next floor to use his telephone. Her hand shaking, she dialed Alphonse Dantan's number at the *Police Judiciare.* Judy had insisted she take the number at the time when the Dantans' home telephone had not yet been installed.

Miri didn't look upon Judy as a special friend, although they had spent many hours drinking hot chocolate together the year before when they were both students and living at the *pension* Fleuris, on *Rue des Ecoles,* and gossiping about their monstrous landlady or the other *pensionnaires.* Miri thought Judy was too frivolous and shallow to be her friend, even though Judy bubbled over with friendliness and even generosity. But she was a philistine.

On the other hand, Miri needed friends, although she was loath to admit it. Her former best friend, Vanessa Tate, an artist, had chilled to her. Miri greatly admired Vanessa as an artist and had enjoyed many hours talking with her about art and men. So she was hurt, more than she would admit, by Vanessa's scornful tone when Miri told her that she had accepted the typing job at FOUSAP. The Army of all places! As a clerk-typist of all things! Miri could not convince her that it was worth it to be able to save enough in a year to go to Spain to paint for ten or twelve months. Vanessa thought that spending a year just to make money was too long to spend away from practicing art full-time. A dedicated artist would have found a more ingenious way to survive. Vanessa's method was to accept a monthly stipend from her rich parents.

Vanessa, currently experimenting with abstract expressionism, had taken an extreme dislike to Miri's attempts at representational painting. (After the murder at *Rue des Ecoles* was solved, a store of documents and photographs left by the Maisel family, who had been deported in 1942, was discovered. Miri had taken old photographs of members of the family and had begun painting from these pictures.)

"Your best work to date was the portrait of Bethel Washton." This was an expressionistic painting along the lines of Max Beckmann, which Miri had done of a Negro actress they had known at Reid Hall, the American University Women's residence in Montparnasse, to which Miri had moved after the murder at the *pension*. "An interesting mixture of expressionist color and cubist form," Vanessa had pronounced on Miri's painting of Bethel Washton.

Miri said nothing in her own defense. She had believed fervently in the Bethel Washton painting as she was doing it, but now that she was doing more representational images, she believed in the new approach she was taking.

Miri's call was picked up at the P.J. switchboard, the errand-boy was sent to inform Dantan that he had a call, and eventually the inspector was on the line.

Miri blurted out the news of her and Kitty's discovery.

"We'll be right over."

After hanging up, Miri sat shivering in Mister Jayes' chair, her teeth chattering. She was petrified in the spot for some time.

By the time she went back down the back stairs to the entry floor, a number of staff had arrived and were being herded together by the uniformed gendarmes sent by Dantan.

3

It was Judy's friend Miri. Breathlessly, she told him that she and another secretary, arriving early at work, had found a body at the foot of the stairs. His head was all bloody; she couldn't tell how it had happened.

Dantan was galvanized.

He quickly filled in Chief Inspector Goulette, dispatched gendarmes to secure the site until the inspectors could get there, and then jumped into a taxi with Jean-Jacques Pilieu to speed to the American-occupied mansion on *Rue Dante*.

Dantan felt a pleasurable thrill at the possibility of a real case. He fervently hoped, if indeed the American lieutenant was truly dead, it was a result of foul play, not just a meaningless accident. And it did not elude him that by the sheer luck that his wife's friend had called him first he might have snatched the case from the Sixth Section, which was usually involved with serious crimes involving foreigners.

Now he could prove his investigative skills. During the *Rue des Ecoles* case he had served merely as an interpreter for the inspectors as they interrogated Americans on the scene. But he had picked up clues from his growing intimacy with one of the American students, Judy Kugel, which contributed to his solving that case. A stroke of luck which led to his promotion to Inspector. This time he would be able to show that he merited it.

In this case, he had already met two of the American soldiers socially, at a dinner of his wife's for a pack of Americans. That might help.

He had become engaged to Judy soon after his promotion, and they were married in April.

As their taxi bumped along the streets, Chief Inspector Goulette expressed concern that the American military would try to keep them out of the investigation. After all, if it was a crime, not an accident, it had taken place in France, not the U.S.A. It was not as though the office was an actual army base, or, as in the case of the American Embassy, considered American soil. And he knew that there was a U.S. Army Criminal Investigation Command (USACIC) with worldwide responsibility, but he did not know how it would affect this case. If it was indeed a crime, it might have been committed either by a member of the military or one of the civilians who worked there.

Goulette thought that if his own investigators quickly gathered forensic evidence, without sacrificing detail, and began their interviews soon, by the time an American investigator arrived from Germany or the States, the French police would have been able to contribute materially to the investigation, and would therefore remain a part of it.

Dantan realized it wouldn't be their case for very long. And he wouldn't be satisfied just to "remain a part of it," he wanted it to be his. If he were to solve it himself it would have to be before the USACIC got there and took over. He did a quick calculation of how much time he might have.

If Dantan were to have any chance of completing the case without the Americans' involvement he would have to move very quickly, and get the P.J.'s own forensic analysis and the medical examiner's report quickly. Very quickly. He was going to try to interview everyone in the office that day, at least superficially.

By the time Miri returned to the foyer, a horde of people was milling around, watched, as best they could, by the gendarmes. Civilian employes had turned up, more than two dozen Americans, as well as a similar number of French nationals, all operators in the basement machine-room, and three or four soldiers.

Colonel Ritchie, in uniform, stood with a commanding bearing near the front door, his eye on the crowd. He had gathered near him his secretary, Kitty Hill, and Sergeant Carr Southwood, the second-highest ranking officer now that Lieutenant Morgan was dead. Kitty Hill was sobbing into a man's handkerchief.

Miri's boss, Charlie Nugent, and his boss, Mr Jayes, stood together, a few feet away from the others. Miri quickly joined them. Charlie kept shaking his head sadly, his chest heaving with deep sighs. Mr Jayes, always rocklike in demeanor at the best of times, was stone-faced.

The medical examiner had now arrived and was scrutinizing the body trying to determine the cause of death. Accidental fall? Stabbing? Bullet-wound? Blunt trauma to the head?

Dantan, Pilieu, and Goulette were accompanied by an extremely thin young man, whom Miri overheard introduced as their interpreter, Armand. This group moved closer to the body. The colonel listened gravely as Armand translated for Chief Inspector Goulette, telling the Americans how they happened to be there and how he proposed to conduct the investigation.

Dantan could have spoken to the colonel directly in English but it was a matter of rank and protocol; the colonel had to be addressed by the chief inspector out of respect.

Dantan took Kitty Hill aside to question her, as the first person on the scene.

Trembling, she poured out her story of finding the lieutenant's body when she unlocked the front door. She was one of the few privileged ones to have a key; the colonel, of course, the lieutenant -- here she sobbed -- and Vic Logan, the civilian manager of the machine-room in the basement, where all the data processing was done. No, she had not seen or heard another soul in the place until Miri Winter arrived soon after she herself did.

Jean-Jacques, who spoke no English, was interviewing Miri without the assistance of Armand, since her French was fluent.

Miri had little more to contribute than Kitty, except that when she had gone up the back stairs she had seen or heard nothing. "I went up the back stairs because I didn't want to go past the body," Miri sobbed, "I used Mr Jayes' phone to call Alphonse -- Inspector Dantan."

It was obvious that Colonel Ritchie wanted no part of the French police. But he had no choice but to cooperate until his own investigating brass got there. He shot Miri a killing look.

Colonel Ritchie sadly looked down at the lieutenant's body and solemnly intoned, "He was a hero in the war. A very brave man. At Anzio he led an assault under heavy enemy fire on a German machine-gun nest he could have delegated to the platoon sergeant, saved many of his men in the bloody battle; and lost a leg there, crawling, bloody, in pain, fortunately he himself was then rescued by the medicos before he bled to death. He got a Bronze Star for that. He had to stay a long stretch in the hospital, and rehabilitation. Then he could have taken retirement at three-quarters pay, as most of those not of the highest rank would do, but the army was his life. He chose to serve however he could, although only at a desk. And then to die like this..... The irony of fighting heroically and surviving grievous wounds, and then to be slain by a common criminal."

Miri hadn't known Lieutenant Morgan had been a hero. She felt very guilty that she hadn't liked him better.

The colonel looked Chief Inspector Goulette in the eye. "I'll set up my command post in the cloakroom on this floor."

Armand duly translated. It was not lost on anyone that the colonel had taken charge.

Colonel Ritchie asked Sergeant Southwood to oversee Privates Parnes and Bernardi in setting up his command post. The cloakroom, off the marble-floored foyer, was small and windowless. It was equipped with a long rack from which American-style wooden hangers dangled, all empty now, since it was mid-summer. There was also a hat rack on the wall, also empty. In one corner of the room was a stack of folding chairs and a folded-up table.

Once the table and about a dozen chairs had been set up, the colonel signalled Craig Jayes and Charlie Nugent to join him in the cloakroom, along with the French inspectors. Then he summoned Kitty and Miri.

Additional police arrived, as well as two photographers with their cumbersome equipment and several forensic technicians carrying their kits. The medical examiner was still on his knees examining the body. A gendarme was keeping everyone at a distance, not that there was much eagerness to get in close and look at the dead man.

The colonel had just begun laying down his rules for the investigation when the doctor came to the door of the cloakroom and signalled the chief inspector, who stepped briefly outside the room with the doctor. The chief inspector returned to the table and whispered something to Armand, who whispered to the colonel. The colonel announced, "It was murder."

Later, Miri learned that the lieutenant had been struck on the head with a blunt weapon. There had been no gunshot or stab-wounds, and the doctor had ruled out an accidental fall.

The colonel asked Kitty to fetch her steno-pad. But the front stairs had been cordoned off by the forensic technicians. She seemed hesitant. Miri, sensing her problem, withdrew a sketch-pad from her voluminous leather handbag, and handed it to Kitty for taking notes.

The colonel announced that he would be contacting USACIC, U.S.Army Criminal Investigation Command, as soon as he could get to his telephone, but to avoid delaying the investigation, he gave permission to the French to pursue their efforts to gather evidence and interview personnel. He made it clear that he thought it was his jurisdiction but would accept whatever help the French could contribute. He did not know how long it would take to get in an officer from USACIC. After all, the victim was "only" a lieutenant.

The colonel laid down a few simple rules for the French investigators.

One. While the French investigators could have a free hand in interviewing any and all personnel at FOUSAP, civilian or military (he would provide Chief Inspector Goulette with a complete list) and in examining the building for evidence, this courtesy did not extend to the contents of any of their files.

Two. Any interviews of himself or the senior civilian administrator, Craig Jayes, were to take place only when Kitty Hill was present to take shorthand notes of the proceedings. He was going to keep Miri Winter on hand, too, for running errands at a moment that a file or something else might be needed.

Miri thought to herself that since they could not yet go upstairs beyond the ground floor there wasn't much she could fetch yet, whatever he might need, since the police were not yet letting them go upstairs.

Three. Any communications about the case would have to be made through him or his designated officer.

Chief Inspector Goulette listened to all this without comment, and when it appeared that the colonel was done, assented with a nod and a polite *"d'accord, Monsieur le Colonel."*

There was no telephone in the cloakroom. Colonel Ritchie was irritated that he could not get to his own offfice. He had important calls to make to HQ. And he wanted to look up all regulations for proper procedures which could pertain to this circumstance. It was very inconvenient that Lieutenant Morgan was the one who had gotten killed, as he was the one the colonel would have turned to for help in seeking out this kind of information.

Kitty had rallied, her eyes red but now dry. She sat very straight, her thick freckled legs crossed, holding Miri's drawing-pad, ready to take down what was said. Miri sat quietly, her large dark eyes were somber.

Through Armand. the chief inspector asked Colonel Ritchie, "Colonel, do you know any reason why Lieutenant Morgan would have come in during the weekend or have stayed late Friday night?"

"Nothing specific, except to say that Lieutenant Morgan could not have been more dedicated to his duty. If something came up that he felt he had to handle off-hours, he wouldn't have hesitated."

"With whom would he have been likely to have some business?"

"Could have been anyone. The lieutenant liked to keep a close watch on things."

"What things?"

"Anything," the colonel said with irritation.

Kitty was taking this all down, dutifully. Armand, the young interpreter, was gaping at her dimpled knees.

The three inspectors quickly agreed to divide the potential interviewees into three groups. The French personnel, who all who worked in the downstairs machine-room, would be the responsibility of Jean-Jacques Pilieu. So would any neighbors or their servants who were still around. The sacred August holiday was almost upon them, and the rich didn't always wait for August to begin their respite from their repose.

Colonel Ritchie and Craig Jayes would be interviewed by Chief Inspector Goulette with Armand's interpreting aid.

Dantan would interview all civilian personnel and noncommissioned officers. Only one private was absent that day, Seymour Levin, said to be in

Garmisch, it was not clear why. The civilians included the assistant civilian supervor, Charles Nugent; Jackie Harris, the archival files manager, all supervisors with reponsibility in the machine-room for keypunching, printing, handling reports and supplies (their underlings were all French, thus the responsibility of Inspector Pilieu); and their manager, Vic Logan, a tense wiry civilian in his late thirties with a sallow complexion and curly black eyelashes. Dantan indicated to Logan that he could now herd this whole crew downstairs.

At last, Colonel Ritchie was allowed into his own office, where he immediately called the brass at HQ to inform them of the crime and to receive instructions. He then had Kitty type up a list of all personnel – military, American civilians, French and other foreign nationals – noting their place in the organization, and the dates their service began, and where.

Miri was delegated to run off twenty copies of this list on ditto-paper, to spare Kitty from exposure to the purple ditto ink, which she intensely disliked. Copies went to each of the French inspectors, to Craig James and Charles Nugent, a number for the files, as well as a supply for the U.S. Army investigators who were expected to turn up.

The colonel set Sergeant Southwood to work on proper procedures for contacting next-of-kin, learning their wishes for disposition of the remains, the shipping of the body back to the States, and who was responsible for arranging a military funeral in these circumstances. He instructed Kitty to find out the details of setting up a memorial service here in Paris, perhaps at the American church, for the FOUSAP personnel and anyone else who knew Morgan and cared to come.

The colonel offered Private Bernardi's assistance to accompany Dantan and Pilieu wherever they went. (He expected the chief inspector to be very much at his own side.) Bernardi obediently tagged along after the men, embarassed to be something of a spy, but he could not understand a word of the French they spoke among themselves.

4

Chief Inspector Goulette (with interpreter Armand by his side) found himself fully occupied with Colonel Ritchie. This left a major portion of the case in Dantan's hands. Pilieu was there too, of course, of course, but he looked to Dantan as the natural leader.

Dantan tried to understand the flow of functions of the office as he undertook more questioning. Dantan and Pilieu started in the basement machine-room.

Restrooms had been installed by the Americans on every floor. None had existed before they took over the building. In the basement, there were restrooms for the use of the workers in the machine-room, so they had no reason to go to any of the floors above, unless summoned by one of the administrators, and they were not encouraged to do so. Of course, they all entered in the morning through the main door on the ground floor.

The paranoia of the Communist-hunting led in the States by Senator Joseph McCarthy, extended to outposts in Europe, too, and the American authorities preferred as little interaction as possible between their American employes and foreign nationals. Dantan was not hopeful of gleaning much, if any, useful information from the French nationals.

According to Vic Logan, he had seen them all out on Friday evening, through the back door in the basement, as he always did, then left himself.

Pilieu began his questioning of the French girls.

Machine-room operations were conducted in two cavernous and windowless rooms lit by fluorescent ceiling fixtures, good for working on documents but mood-depressing. The manager had his own small office on the floor, and just outside it was his secretary's desk and typewriter.

Vic Logan took charge of the detectives and gave them a quick tour of the operation.

The keypunchers' job was to take the hand-written reports from various sources and transfer or "punch" the data into machines that created little holes in special cards and then automatically stacked the cards in racks. The verifiers' work was outwardly indistinguishable from that of the keypunchers; their job was to keypunch the same data, but with a deck of already outputted keypunched cards run by the machine to compare the two outputs. Any discrepancies between the first deck and the second, were cast into a separate slot, and would have to be reconciled manually.

Carolene Mayce, the keypunch-supervisor, was a rigid woman with bleached bouffant hair and big teeth. Together, she and the verifying-supervisor, Harriet Barlow, a plump jolly-looking woman, were in charge of resolving any discrepancies. If they could not do so, it became Vic Logan's job.

There were several burly fellows who were printer-operators. Their principal assignment was to feed decks of cards into the hoppers for printing; to make sure each of the large clacking printers did not run out of paper; and to lug boxes of paper or cards from one venue to another.

Logan displayed his short temper when Dantan said he wanted to ask him some questions. But he waved the inspector to his desk beside the doorway connecting the two machine-rooms from which he could strategically observe the entire operation. His steel desk held a green-shaded desk-lamp, and many many printouts.

Just outside his office sat his secretary. Marjory Young was a small wan young woman who gave Dantan a feeble smile. Logan dismissed any interest Dantan might have in wasting time questioning her, assuring the detective that she knew nothing.

But Dantan liked interviewing people who supposedly "knew nothing," often this was a mischaracterization. He would talk to Marjory Young.

Logan was impatient, he had work to do, they were behind because of the earlier disruption. He seemed angrier at the disruption to his schedule than at the fact that an officer had been murdered!

But Dantan patiently explained that he considered it imperative to understand the operations of the office.

Logan begrudgingly told him the basics of what this group was doing. In order to create giant master reports for Washington it consolidated financial reports from various U.S. finance offices around Europe for the expenses related to the Army. In brief, it reported what each base was spending, and on what; what funds were being disbursed to local agencies, what materiel had been purchased or supplied, and to what organizations it was shipped.

"These reports come to you on paper and your office keypunches them in?"

"No, no," Logan said impatiently, "regional reports come in on cards, together with a paper run. The keypunching done here is from information sources in France, and for reconciliation purposes." He made a dismissive gesture.

"All the personnel in your section are civilians?"

"Yes, the French nationals working on keypunch and verification, and the American supervisors."

"No military?"

"A couple of privates who hang around," Logan said scornfully, "but they serve no useful purpose that I can see."

"Where are they now?"

Logan shrugged. "Probably circling the wagons. The less I see of any of them, the better, anyway." He gave a contemptuous glance in the direction of Private Bernardi, who had been sent downstairs to offer any assistance, and was trying to chat with two of the French girls.

"Where is the entrance normally used by the employees in this section?" Dantan asked.

Logan sighed, resigned that he would not get rid of the detective immediately. "They're supposed to enter in the morning by the front door, then come down the back stairs, but in fact, the first one to arrive unlocks the back door, which is a shortcut for those who work on this floor, and they troop in that way. Leaving for the day or for lunch they go out the back and as I am always the last one here, I lock the back door, then go up to the ground floor and leave by the front door."

"There are two doors in total? Or any others?"

"Just the two, the front door which opens on to the foyer on the ground floor, and the back door here in the basement."

"Who besides yourself has a key to the back door?"

" Colonel Ritchie, of course. The lieutenant did too."

"And Kitty Hill?"

"No, but I believe she has a key to the front door."

"Does anyone from your unit ever have reason to go to either of the upper floors?"

"Naturally. There may be reports to be brought up to the lieutenant or the colonel on the first floor, and since on the second floor is a combined files-room and conference-room, documents are often brought there. On a schedule, older reports are filed upstairs. The dumb-waiter is used for bulk, but often, when fewer documents are required, for example, for a meeting in the conference-room, one of the huskier types here carries the necessary cartons of printouts up to the second floor, brings them back down when the meeting is done, unless they are to be left in the files-room for filing away there. Foreign nationals are not encouraged to go above the ground floor."

"*Monsieur* Logan, what time did you leave the building on Friday evening?"

"About seven-thirty, more or less. Not unusal for me."

"Did you return to the building at any time during the weekend?"

"No siree! I put in enough time Monday to Friday!"

"Was anyone still in the building when you left on Friday?"

"Not that I know of. None of my people were, I saw them leave myself. As for any others, I can only tell you I didn't hear sounds of life, and when I went to the courtyard to get my car there were no other cars parked there. Of course, I wouldn't know if anyone were still parked in the backyard since I had no occasion to look. It's not heavily utilized. I think the only ones who use it regularly are the colonel and Sergeant Carr Southwood, who doesn't want any scratches on his precious Caddy, and you won't catch him working a minute late, not that he does much when he is around. Arrogant bastard. Father owns half the steel business in Pittsburgh, and the sergeant acts as if it's all his doing. And Jackie Harris, when she brings her truck in, parks back there. A 1953 red Mercury truck, V-8 and the new automatic transmission, weighs almost a ton. I don't know if she did so Friday evening."

Dantan had seen a large light-blue Cadillac in the courtyard. The Americans certainly liked their cars to stand out in a city of small black autos, bicycles and Velo-Solexes. He smiled at recalling seeing the American boxer, Sugar Ray Robinson, cruising around Paris in his lavendar Cadillac convertible, a familiar sight to Parisians. But the Parisians had a soft spot for Sugar Ray, very different from their feelings for other Americans driving monstrous cars. He could only imagine how they reacted to a red one-ton truck -- driven by a woman!

Dantan thanked Logan for his time, informing him he wanted to interview the American civilians in his group, and would do so upstairs in the administrators' offices. Logan assented with a curt nod.

Dantan felt pressure to hurry; pressure he was putting on himself because he so urgently wanted to solve the case before the American investigators arrived. He hoped to cover all the interviews that day and study the reports from forensics and the doctor and come up with a plausible hypothesis by the time the American investigators got down to work.

The forensic technicians had completed their work on the marble stairs, but John Morgan's body, covered with a sheet, still lay sprawled at the bottom of the staircase.

On the first floor, Colonel Ritchie was sitting stiffly behind his desk, his secretary Kitty Hill was flitting back and forth with documents and coffee, and Messrs Jayes and Nugent had returned to their offices and each sat somewhat immobilized behind his desk. Dantan gave them an abbreviated idea of his planned activities for that day.

On this floor were also rest-rooms marked "Gentlemen" and "Ladies," installed, like the others, by the Americans. When this building had been a luxurious private mansion, the distinguished residents had used chamber-pots, the slops emptied by servants.

Dantan stoppped in to use the mens' room on this floor, and seeing the gleaming fixures and mirrors got a sudden insight into why his father-in-law had made such an issue of the bathroom construction for the newlyweds' apartment.

A moment later, Private Bernardi entered to use the facilities. He seemed so nervous and anxious that Dantan decided to interview him quickly.

Dantan recalled the one time he had previously met Private Bernardi. It had been at his wife's dinner party back in May, for a pack of Americans. Bernardi at that time had been exceedingly jovial, in fact one of the others said his nickname was "jolly green giant." He had guffawed heartily at any nonsense that was said, and his laugh was so contagious that everyone, or at least the Americans, laughed along with him and thought they were having a good time.

And now, here was this large man trembling like a bowl of jelly, his eyes reflecting fear or anxiety. Dantan would question him shortly.

Dantan proceeded up to the second floor.

The second floor consisted of an immense salon with a vaulted twenty-foot-high ceiling. The salon's design suggested that it had once been two rooms. By the back stairs were several small offices, also with high ceilings. A dumbwaiter opened into one of them.

These offices could conceivably have once been one room, perhaps a serving-pantry. The salon was a stunning area, its high ceiling elaborately painted in a gridlike pattern with putti and flowers and other intricate images. Clearly, it had been the ballroom or grand salon when the mansion was a private residence. All four walls were covered in mirrors, floor to ceiling.

What had once undoubtedly been furnished with a resplendence of gilt-adorned carved ballroom chairs, lavish draperies, and richly woven Persian carpets of intricate design (just the sort of thing his mother-in-law had in mind for Judy's and his apartment!), had been redecorated by the U.S. Army. The floor was now covered in tough gray carpet, probably protecting fine parquet floors. Down the center of the room was a long formica conference table; sixteen austere, straight-backed chairs, several of them pushed askew, circled the table. Around three of the walls were filing cabinets, floor to ceiling. They were wide enough to accommodate the large printouts. Dantan observed that the file cabinets had not been pushed up against the walls, but were set forward about a meter-and-a-half. Dantan felt a moment of gratitude for the sensitivity of the Americans, who had obviously shown care and concern for these rooms, in contrast to their paving over the backyard garden.

Three of the small offices contained two metal desks each; a third one, one. A metal nameplate proclaimed this desk to be occupied by J. Harris. The other offices belonged to Sergeant Carr Southwood, Private Peter Parnes, Private Dennis Bernardi, and Private Seymour Levin. None were in their offices.

All the desks were whistle-clean. The sergeant's desk had a telephone on it; the others did not. Private Levin was out of the city and had been, presumably, during the weekend.

Above the second floor were what had formerly been servants' quarters, or *chambres de bonne.* They were tiny and had low slanted roofs. They couldn't have been very comfortable for the servants who had lived there and who had maintained this place in the days of its former magnificence. Now the small rooms were used by the Americans to store a miscellany of boxes of all sizes, some with markings identifying them as originating at the PX.

Dantan did not believe the murderer could be anyone other than FOUSAP personnel, either military or civilian. Anyone within could have gained access, but an outsider would have been questioned immediately, as FOUSAP had no civilian visitors.

Now that he understood the layout of the mansion, Dantan was ready to resume questioning. As a courtesy he would have begun with the assistant senior civilian supervisor, Charles Nugent. But he saw that he and Craig Jayes were with Colonel Ritchie in the latter's office. He took the opportunity to begin with Private Bernardi, whose demeanor he had found suspicious.

Private Bernardi was even more nervous than Dantan had observed him to be earlier.

Dantan pressed him to describe his movements Friday night. He spoke hesitantly, haltingly, as if he were listening to his own words as he spoke, to make sure he didn't give something away. He had permission from Carolyn Mayce to borrow her car for the weekend, she had given him the keys during the day, and he took right off at five-thirty. He wanted to see Chartres.

"That seems exceedingly generous of her," Dantan said skeptically.

"I've done enough for her."

"What favors did you do for Madame Mayce that would warrant her lending you her car?"

Private Bernardi shrugged. "You'll find out soon enough, I expect."

And you drove to Chartres that night?"

"Yes."

"Where did you stay overnight?"

"Slept in the car to save money."

Private Bernardi was sweating profusely.

"When did you leave Chartres?"

"Saturday afternoon."

"Then where did you go?"

"Back to Paris. Didn't do much."

Dantan mulled over this: all the questions had been innocuous, and Bernardi's replies had been unexceptionable. Yet the man was squirming.

"Did you return to the FOUSAP office at any time during the weekend?"

"Why would I want to do that? No, I didn't."

Sergeant Southwood, whom Dantan interviewed next, readily admitted that he had gone to the PX immediately leaving work, at five-thirty. But he was evasive about the rest of his weekend.

"Purely personal, Inspector," he said. "Of no relevance to your investigation."

Dantan did not press the point. He could always get back to the sergeant later if something came up.

The questioning of Private Parnes, a slim smiling young man, was perfunctory. Private Parnes had left work promptly at five-thirty on Friday and driven directly to the PX. Charlie Nugent, his roommate, had accompanied him. The had gone shopping for food for the weekend. Charlie was an excellent cook. They didn't like French food; too many sauces.

The only person who had admitted to departing later than five-thirty on Friday was Vic Logan. It would have been odd if he had not, as he was known to work late often.

5

Miri was bursting with a secret she thought could be a clue to the murder. When Jean-Jacques Pilieu had questioned her she had told him nothing about it. She knew that the colonel was already furious at her for bringing in French investigators and that he wanted the personnel to tell them as little as possible. But Miri did feel somewhat of an obligation to tell Dantan what she knew, since she had brought him in and therefore ought to help him if she could. Besides, he was practically a friend, as the husband of a person who wanted to be her friend.

She asked Charlie's advice on her dilemma. Dantan was in with Mister Jayes; she presented Charlie with her problem. But when she told him her big "secret," it turned out that he already knew all about what was going on and assured her that it would be all right to tell the French inspectors, and in fact would be better, so that if they found out some other way, it wouldn't look as if the Americans were trying to cover up anything.

Therefore, when Dantan joined Charlie and was told to see Miri first, she was prepared to tell him everything.

She said breathlessly, "It occurred to me after Jean-Jacques questioned me that I know something that might be a clue."

Dantan sat on the straight-backed chair Charlie lounged in when he wanted to explain, in a leisurely way, something he wanted Miri to do, or simply to share some new tidbit of gossip with her. Dantan encouraged her to continue.

"When I first started working here at FOUSAP, Carolene Mayce, the keypunching supervisor, came around acting friendly. She was wearing a really tight corset and her bleached bouffant hair was sprayed so stiff I didn't think we would get along, but I hardly knew a soul in the office, so I tried to keep an open mind.

"Carolene offered to drive me to the PX and show me around. She had driven her own car in that day so we could go there together right after work. I was really grateful, because I hadn't seen the PX yet, and everybody talked about what they had gotten there.

"When we left that day Private Dennis Bernardi was waiting for us in the courtyard near Carolene's big blue car. It turned out he would be getting a ride to the PX too, but once we got there he melted into the crowd.

"The PX turned out to be a fascinating place, a huge room with all kinds of stuff, French clothing, and books, as well as fresh food. They had American cleaning-powders which are much better than the French, and real toilet paper, not the slimy little sheets the French use. I could even have afforded to start smoking again, American cigarettes were so cheap, but I decided not to, in case I left this job and had to pay European prices again. They carried peanut-butter, a real treat I hadn't been able to find anywhere, and odd pieces of French couturier clothes, very cheap. They were mostly too small for me, though, really tiny sizes. Carolene said they were probably samples from previous fashion shows, as the designers didn't make ready-to-wear.

"There were a few pieces, very dressy, in huge sizes. Carolene thought these might have been made for rich clients who had changed their minds.

"Carolene and I browsed through the clothing racks for awhile, even though nothing looked as if it would fit either of us, but it was fun. I did spot a black mohair coat that flaired out, and tried it on right there, and it practically fit if I could move the buttons, but I couldn't bring myself to spend that much money on something I didnt really need. My French-schoolboy cape was warm enough. They had a few books too. I found a copy of T.S.Eliot's *Old Possum's Book of Practical Cats* in the children's section.

"Then Carolene got impatient, and told me why she was really there. To pick up her daily allowance of a quart of Scotch. I couldn't believe she would drink that much, but she laughed and said she didn't drink it, she sold it to French bars. She also picked up cartons of American cigarettes and sold those too.

"It turned out that Carolene wanted me to buy a daily bottle of Scotch too, and sell it through her. She would give me part of the profit. I refused. Carolene was miffed. After that, she never offered to drive me to the PX again. It turned out that Dennis Bernardi had also bought a bottle of Scotch and put it carefully in Carolene's huge trunk along with her other booty. He may have seen how shocked I was, because he made a point of telling me that he was not profiting from the Scotch, he was buying it for Carolene who would make the profit. They had an arrangement that once he had bought a certain number of bottles and cartons of cigarettes for her business he could borrow her car for a whole weekend."

"If Carolene was so open about telling you of this black market operation," Dantan asked, "then

others in the office must know about it. Do you know
who else is doing that?"

"As far as I know, some of the oafs in the machine-room, Barney, Al, Eddie and Terk. And
Carolene of course."

"And Private Dennis Bernardi," Dantan pointed
out.

"But he isn't profiting from it." Miri felt bad about
bringing Dennis into it. He was a big hulk of a
sweetie.

"He's getting a *quid pro quo.* The use of a car."
And that seemed strange to Dantan, picking up a
few bottles of liquor per week and some cigarettes
in exchange for the car. Unless something else was
involved....

"Is *Monsieur* Logan involved too?"

"I don't think so. He's always busy working,
stays late a lot, and doesn't seem to socialize with
anyone. His wife went Stateside back in March because of some family medical emergency. That's how
I got my job. She was the clerk-typist for Mr Jayes
and Charlie, and they didn't want to wait for the
States to send them someone that they might not
even like, so they decided to hire locally. There are
lots of American girls, like the ones at Reid Hall,
who are just panting to get a job in Paris when their
third year of college abroad is up and they would
have to go home and finish their fourth year there."

Dantan dropped in on Charlie Nugent to verify Miri's tale. He asked Charlie if he knew anything about staff liquor purchases on a big scale that they then sold on the black market.

Charlie said mildly, "As far as I know, they are not doing anything illegal, just purchasing their liquor allowance, and some cigarettes. What they do with it after that is their business."

Dantan was surprised that Nugent, knowing what was going on, took such a casual attitude toward it.

"They load up every single day!"

Charlie shrugged. "If they were breaking any rules you can be sure I would hear about it. And action would be taken."

"Could the lieutenant have been pressuring them to stop, perhaps threatening them with some kind of punishment?"

Dantan found it difficult to think that the lieutenant would be coming down hard on this black-marketing group when their own civilian boss was treating it so lightly. But he wouldn't let it drop just yet.

"Punishing for what? No regulations were broken. Lieutenant Morgan, or any other officer, couldn't punish someone for actions that were merely unethical or that he personally disapproved of. Besides," Charlie added, "if it keeps staff happy enough to do their job here, far away from their homes and families...." He shrugged.

"You yourself don't do this special shopping at
the PX?"

Charlie grinned calmly. "Oh no. I'm past the
age of hustling. I don't even shop there. I leave that
to my roommate, Peter Parnes, who is a lot younger
and stronger and more energetic than I am. I can
vouch for him, that he's not engaged in anything
shady, or even unethical. He's simple and honest.
He works upstairs in Files."

Dantan had already interviewed Private Parnes,
and considered Nugent's assessment of him reasonable.

"It seems that almost every supervisor reporting to Vic Logan is engaged in this black
marketeering," Dantan said mildly. "Do you think
Vic Logan himself is too?"

"I would be extremely surprised to hear that he
is. He works very hard here, and puts in long hours
of his own volition. Since his wife left for the States
back in March he works even harder. Marianne. She
was a sweetheart. She was our typist, you know. But
her mother became deathly ill and she was given
indefinite leave without pay. But at the time it didn't
seem she was likely to return to her job. That's why
we hired Miri. Had to have a typist, and someone
hired locally could be brought on much quicker,
without relocation expenses, and dispensed with
much more easily in case Marianne did come back.

Still doesn't look like she's going to."

Miri, who was listening through the open door between her office and Charlie's, was certainly relieved to hear that, she didn't want to be "dispensed with" until she was ready to be! Six or seven months more and she would have saved enough to live in Spain for a year and paint.

"What can you tell me about the civilian personnel under Logan?"

"Tony Alotta, the printing supervisor, is always dashing off to the races. Auteuil. Longchamps. His girlfriend is Harriet Barlow, head of Verifying. They don't do the liquor runs, they just like to guzzle! And then they're off again to the races. Far as I know the print-operators, Barney, Terk, Al and Eddie are doing the daily Scotch pick-ups at the PX along with Carolene."

"That's helpful," Dantan said mildly. "Do you know of anything the lieutenant was handling that would have someone very very angry at him? Or fearful of him?"

Charlie shook his head. "Nothing that I know about. He was not well-liked, very straitlaced and humorless, but not the type to arouse the kind of fury that leads to murder. I doubt if it had anything to do with this liquor thing. Talk to the colonel's secretary, Kitty Hill, though. She was around him a lot more, and she's a nosey parker anyway, she might be able to tell you something."

"The lieutenant had no friends at all?"

"Well, as to what he was doing on the outside, I couldn't say. He did have a somewhat odd, I don't know if you could call it friendship, connection with a private, very unusual for officers to associate with mere soldiers, especially the lowliest. He played chess an evening or two a week with Private Seymour Levin. That seems to have come about when the lieutenant heard of Levin's reputation as a crack chess-player at Garmisch. The lieutenant himself was supposedly an excellent player, and invited Private Levin to a game. It became a regular thing."

"Is there a possibility that this Jackie Harris could be part of the liquor black-marketeering? After all, she does have that capacious truck."

"Anything is possible, but I never heard a word breathed about her. Besides, she is genuinely obsessed with buying big bulky old furniture and is forever lugging it from unlikely places to her barnlike apartment. That's what the truck is for.

"She is tracking down every piece of Biedermeier furniture in Europe, flea markets, antique shops, auctions, and storing her finds in a huge delapidated apartment near *Châtelet*, then she'll let Uncle Sam pay the costs of shipping it all back to the States when her tour is up, as household effects, you know. Plans to open an antique shop in Atlanta. From what I've heard," he chuckled, "a shop won't be big enough, she'll need a whole warehouse!

"Dennis Bernardi is besotted with her, follows her everywhere! She's a real character in her own way. Nuts about cars. She can strip down an engine, clean it, get it going faster than any man or boy." He chuckled. "Some of the guys think of her as one of the boys." Charlie grinned, and said with some satisfaction, "Yes, we're an interesting crew. The lieutenant was a hero at Anzio..." Charlie gave a big sigh. "It's ironic that he survived the war, although badly wounded, and then he gets murdered here in a peaceful backwater office. Then there's Miri, our typist, an artist, really. But I guess you know about that, don't you? She told me she is friends with your wife."

"Yes, she's a serious artist. She gave us one of her paintings as a wedding gift, and it is very charming."

Dantan thanked Charlie Nugent, then made his downstairs to the basement to talk with Vic Logan again.

Logan already knew about the black market activities of some of his personnel, but shrugged it off. "We have too much work to do here without looking for trouble where there isn't any."

"Might the lieutenant have taken a less tolerant view?"

"No doubt he did. He was not exactly a tolerant guy. But what could he have done? They weren't going against any regulations. I doubt if he was try-

ing to impose his stricter ethical code on them."
Logan reached for some papers on his desk, and
began studying them. It was a dismissal, and since
Dantan had no further questions for Logan at this
time, he merely indicated that he wanted to interview the various supervisors, and Logan waved him
along.

Back up to the first floor, where the machine-
room supervisors were waiting in Mr Jayes' office,
Dantan began interviewing Carolene Mayce first.
She was a formidable-looking woman in a tight
girdle. It was easy to see her make the young girls
working under her cower.

Carolene Mayce told Dantan that she had left
promptly at five-thirty on Friday in a crowd along
with everyone else from the machine-room, exiting
through the basement door.

"Did you go straight home?"

"No. Dennis Bernardi had borrowed my car
over the weekend. I went off with someone."

Dantan did not ask whom. He suspected it
would be easy enough to find that out without an-
tagonizing Madame Mayce.

"To purchase a quart of Scotch?"

Carolene colored but answered without hesitation, "That's right. My legal allowance, Inspector."

"Did Lieutenant Morgan ever speak to you
about these purchases?"

"He spoke to everyone about everything. He

was always trying to make sure everybody was behaving."

"And were they?"

"As far as I know."

"Do you have any idea why anyone would want to go so far as to kill him?"

"I really don't. He was self-righteous and humorless but that's hardly a motive."

Carolene had seen or heard nothing unusual that Friday evening, and had not returned to the office at any time during the weekend. She had no theories about the murder.

"That was very generous of you to lend your car to Private Bernardi...."

"He does things for me too, sometimes. He always returns the car clean inside and out, with a full gas-tank."

"What else does he do?"

She turned her head away.

Dantan got very similar responses from each of the other supervisors and print-operators. They had gone to the PX to get their liquor allowances, leaving the office exactly at five-thirty. Tony Alotta and Harriet Barlow had driven right out to the track to catch the last races, and had noticed nothing all day that seemed unusual.

Vic Logan's secretary, Marjory Young, was a shy thin blonde girl very upset over the murder and clearly nervous about being interviewed. She kept blinking rapidly, and kept patting her hair as she spoke. "I really don't know anything," she murmured. Just what her boss had said.

"Do you recall anything different on Friday?"

"Nothing. I'm sorry. Only that Mister Logan was even more short-tempered than usual, not that he is ever nice about things. But once Lieutenant Morgan came downstairs and asked to look at some stuff, Mr Logan started screaming at me and everyone."

"More than usual?"

"Maybe not more. He has a terrible temper. I've been wanting to get a transfer because he gets me so upset most of the time but I've been afraid if I asked for a one he would give me a bad performance rating and spoil my chances of getting accepted anywhere else. Maybe now with the murder and all they will understand more about me wanting a transfer and it won't look as if I'm trying to get away from Mr Logan, only scared about hanging around here."

"*Mlle* Young, what time did you leave on Friday?"

"Five-thirty, same as everyone else from the machine-room. Mister Logan often grumbles that I haven't gotten all my work done by the end of the day, but he's never asked me to stay late to finish anything because he didn't want an appearance of impropriety. But often I would find a pile of extra work in the morning."

"This morning too?"

"Not today."

"Do you remember seeing everyone leave at the same time on Friday?"

"I guess so. I didn't take special notice. It seemed like aways. Mr Logan let us out, then went back to his desk." By now she was openly smiling at him and patting her hair.

Dantan thanked her, then sought Jackie Harris, who was now in her office.

She was sitting primly at her desk, turning the pages of a bound data printing. Small, thin, dark, with sharp features, she had a pointed nose, a pointed chin, even her ears were slightly pointed. And she had a sharp manner about her too.

"*Mlle* Harris, were you in the office any time over the weekend?"

Jackie gave a brittle laugh. "Inspector, I was in Germany all weekend, buying antiques as I often do."

""What time did you leave this building Friday night?"

She hesitated, then said, "A little after five-thirty."

"Who else was still here when you left?"

"I saw no one. But Vic Logan often works late. He may still have been here, I wouldn't know. I never go down to his Hades."

"What day and time was it when you arrived back in Paris?"

"Oh, late Sunday."

Dantan next met with Inspector Pilieu. Pilieu had conducted interviews among the neighbors. The owners, he had learned from servants at each of the houses, had already left for summer vacations. A housekeeper next door had been shaking a dustmop in the backgarden and had noticed the big red truck parked in the Americans' backyard. But that was during the day, she knew nothing of what had happened later. The gardener at the same house had been watering plants in the late afternoon, and had noticed several autos in the back parking-lot, not unusual, and, he seemed to recall, the red truck, but had no other information to offer.

The only servant at the house on the other side was the chauffeur, who admitted that he took a great interest in all the vehicles the Americans parked in the front courtyard and in the backyard. He thought that by six o'clock, perhaps earlier, they were all gone except for the brown Dodge. The light blue Cadillac departed along with all the others. The driver was accompanied by a woman, perhaps the one who usually drove a blue Buick, but he wasn't sure. He seemed to recall that the brown Dodge left sometime later, then returned, well after all the others had gone.

Chief Inspector Goulette had more or less given up getting any hard information from the colonel, who was intent on seeming to cooperate while really offering no information at all.

Dantan went to question Kitty Hill. She was in her own little office, sorting papers in a desultory way, and welcomed Dantan's interruption.

"Can you think of anyone who had a grudge against Lieutenant Morgan? Or was really angry at him?"

"Nobody really liked him, I'm afraid, although I admired him and wished he would have loosened up. He didn't like kidding. I'm not sure he even understood it. He was tough on people, but fair. I can't think of anyone who would want to kill him."

"Had he any friends among the personnel here?"

"I didn't see any, except that he played chess sometimes with Private Levin, only because he had heard the private was such a terrific player. The colonel thought the lieutenant should have been able to find an officer who could play chess but he didn't. The game became a frequent thing whenever Private Levin was around. He travels back and forth more than any private I've ever seen. He's in Garmisch right now. They would play at some *café*. The colonel was not happy that the lieutenant was fraternizing with a non-commissioned G.I., but he looked the other way because the lieutenant was otherwise perfectly correct."

Dantan, with a smile and a twinkle in his eye, asked her, "And what about you? Who are your special friends here?"

To his astonishment, Kitty Hill turned beet-red.

Dantan went back down to the machine-room to speak with Vic Logan again. He was more impatient than ever.

"Monsieur Logan, you had indicated on Friday night you had worked until around seven-thirty?"

"That's right."

""But didn't you leave much earlier, and then return to the office before leaving at seven-thirty?"

Logan was silent for a moment. "I guess that's right. I had forgotten. I went out for a quick bite to eat, and then came back to work some more."

"Where did you eat?"

"Where did I eat?"

"That's right."

"Some bistro in the neighborhood, I never noticed its name."

"But you could point it out if Inspector Pilieu were to accompany you?"

"What the hell is this? Some kind of grilling?"

"Just collecting facts, *Monsieur* Logan. Please do not be offended."

Dantan reacted to Logan's defensiveness. Was there a reason for it? Or was it just Logan's general cantankerousness?

Dantan shifted to more neutral ground. "Do any of the soldiers help down here?"

"Help? Ha! Hinder would be more like it. Private Levin is usually getting in the way when he's in town, mercifully that's not all the time. And the sergeant thinks it's his duty to keep tabs on us and likes to ask officious uninformed questions."

"Maybe he wants to feel useful?"

"Useful? I doubt that he cares about that. He's a selfish bastard."

"So he wasn't around here at five-thirty on Friday?"

"No."

Dantan thanked him and once more sought out Kitty Hill in her office. She had calmed down from her momentary embarassment.

"*Mlle* Hill, you're in a unique position to have insights into the personnel. I'd like you to tell me whatever you feel you can about the soldiers here."

"You mean gossip?"

That was exactly what Dantan meant, but he wanted to couch the request in more dignified terms. "Let's just say, informal observations."

"I don't mind," she murmured.

"Private Peter Parnes?"

"A sweet nothing. Charlie Nugent's roommate."

"Private Dennis Bernardi?"

"A big dumb lug. He's infatuated with cars and Jackie Harris." She giggled.

"Private Seymour Levin?"

"The lieutenant liked him, for some unknown

reason. They would play chess together sometimes. It gave Private Levin a swelled head. Thought he could just drop in on the colonel to talk to him sometimes, but the colonel looked on the privates as low-life and would tell him to get lost and take his concerns to Sergeant Southwood."

"What about Sergeant Southwood?"

Kitty smiled mischievously. She had charming dimples. "His family is very rich and his father has connections. He could have gotten some cushy assignment, like driving some general's wife around, but he preferred to hide out here."

"Do you know why?" Dantan had a feeling there was little Kitty didn't know, if she cared to tell.

Another mischievous smile. "He likes to do certain things. Paris is a good place for him."

"Oh?"

Kitty lowered her already soft voice conspiratorially. "Don't tell anyone, promise? Only Charlie Nugent knows. And Carolene Mayce, of course."

"I promise."

"He likes to dress up like a woman." She put a finger to her lips. "He goes to special clubs on weekends."

"How did Madame Mayce come to know?" Dantan could see Kitty Hill sharing gossip with Charlie Nugent, but he didn't see her having a rapport with Madame Mayce.

"Oh, she goes with him. She likes to dress up like a man. They're a regular couple." Kitty smirked. "He buys men's clothes for her at the PX, and she buys women's things for him. Nobody is supposed to know. But I've seen them shopping together several times. He holds the man's jacket for her to try on, she holds up the gown or dress to see if it would fit him. I told Charlie about it, and he said my theory sounded right. But he wouldn't tell. The colonel and the lieutenant are very straitlaced about what they think is immoral, namely almost everything."

The recreational activities of the various personnel were becoming clearer and clearer to Dantan, but he didn't see that the information was of any use in his murder investigation.

Pilieu came to inform him that the chief inspector wanted them to leave for a meeting as soon as Dantan felt ready. He did. Although he had questioned everyone as he had intended, he had no strong hypothesis. He did want to talk things over with his chief. And if the technicians had turned up any forensic evidence yet, of course he wanted to hear about it together with the medical examiner's report.

6

At the end of the working day, cronies huddled in small groups, brought together by the tragedy. Except for Dennis, who had taken off early, Miri had no one to huddle with: her own fault. She had rejected the friendship, the one with strings attached, offered by Carolene Mayce; Kitty Hill was out of the question; Vic Logan's secretary, Marge, was a cowering wimp.

Miri would have liked to be part of the French keypunch girls' group, but they were not friendly even though her French was excellent. They resented the fact that their salaries were a fraction of what the American girls got, even though they had to know English, while their American co-workers didn't have to know French.

They couldn't even accuse the Americans of treating them unfairly; their own government had ruled that French nationals working for foreigners (that is, Americans, as nobody else was hiring) had to be paid along the French pay-scale, so that French workers would not desert their jobs in French establishments to all go work for the Americans. It was a formidable barrier to the forming of close friendships. The American command was just as happy about it anyway.

For once she wished that Seymour Levin was in town. Her feelings about the large calm bearlike young man were very mixed: she admired him, she felt very good with him until he started getting closer and closer and touching her all over. That made her nervous, although it did feel good too. On the whole, she was less in turmoil when he was on one of his trips to Germany looking into things, when they wrote intellectual letters to each other. But now it would have been comforting to have him around. No matter what she said on any subject, he seemed to find it interesting.

She kept going over in her mind the different people who worked at FOUSAP, and couldn't imagine any of them actually killing anyone. The most arrogant and nasty was Sergeant Carr Southwood. He drove around in a huge Cadillac paid for by his rich parents, trying to scare people into thinking they were going to get run over. He was always saying hurtful things to anyone who annoyed him in the slightest, but that didn't mean he would hurt someone physically. There were some big and burly guys in the machine-room, but size didn't mean the person was a killer. Look at Dennis. Huge, but an utter pussycat. It was terrifying to think that someone among them was and she had no idea who it could be.

Miri rarely felt lonesome, rarely felt the need for the company of another human being, but she did now.

At least Judy Dantan would find it fascinating to hear about what had happened, if her husband hadn't told her already. Chances are he wouldn't have. He was really busy with the investigation. Miri walked to the *café* near the Metro where she sometimes had her morning coffee, bought a *jeton* and placed her call from the public telephone in the back.

"Miri! Great to hear from you!"

"Alphie didn't tell you what happened?"

"Something awful?" Judy sounded alarmed.

Miri related the events of the day.

"Come right over!" Judy ordered. "We'll have a some iced chocolate and you can tell me all about it. You must be all shook up."

Miri admitted that she was frightened. "But I have to do some painting first."

"Then come for dinner. That way both you and Alphie can tell me everything. And Germaine is making roast beef, string beans and mashed potatoes. I taught her how and she beats them up fluffy as whipped cream."

Miri looked forward to that.

Miri thought about Lieutenant Morgan. They had had very little contact since the day when he, with Mister Jayes and Charlie Nugent, had interviewed her for the clerk-typist position. At the time she didn't like him; he seemed humorless and strict.

Seymour had arranged the interview. When he heard that Marianne Logan was suddenly leaving her job to return to the States, he spoke to Mister Jayes about interviewing Miri for the job. By the time Seymour mentioned Miri to them, the civilian bosses, Craig Jayes and Charlie Nugent, had interviewed fifty-seven girls. None had gotten past Charlie, to whom the clerk-typist would be reporting directly. Gigglers made him nervous, those who seemed like chatter-boxes might pair up with Kitty Hill and unmercifully drive him crazy, and then there were those who couldn't type at all, even at the snail's pace required by the job, or couldn't spell. Unaccountably, he liked Miri and wanted to hire her. By then, Mister Jayes would have agreed to hire a chimpanzee if it could type.

The colonel's secretary, Kitty Hill, was starting to complain of overwork, as she was used to doing almost nothing except making her rounds and chatting, and now she was daily typing two or three endorsements (short messages preceded and followed by lengthy military titles and organizations)for Mister Jayes and Charlie Nugent. This was work that Miri, or whoever they hired, would be typing.

The colonel was all set to approve hiring Miri as soon as Mister Jayes spoke with him after the interview. But his aide, Lieutenant Morgan, was not as easy to win over.

Lieutenant Morgan was mistrustful of Miri when he learned that she was fluent in French. This raised a question in his mind about her loyalty. His suspicion was further aroused by her response to what he thought was his most important question.

As part of his screening interview, he had passed across the desk a piece of paper which, he said, contained a list of numerous organizations. He told her to look at the list carefully and check off any groups to which she had ever been a member.

Instead of looking at the list, which was densely printed with what seemed like hundreds of names, Miri handed it back to him with a laugh, saying, "I don't have to look at this to know I never belonged to any of them. I am not a joiner and the only thing I ever belonged to was the Girl Scouts."

Instead of letting it go at that, the lieutenant frowned and perused the list. It was, he informed her, a list of subversive Communist-infiltrated organizations.

"Aha!" Sure enough, he had found the Girl Scouts on the list! The Girl Scouts was considered a subversive organization, because of its International Friendship badge. The implication was that the scout who worked for this kind of badge might feel too friendly toward some Communist country.

Miri suppressed the urge to laugh and said soberly, "I never went for the International Friendship badge, and I was eleven years old when I was a Girl Scout. I never even made First Class because once I did the arts and crafts badges, I got bored and dropped out." She didn't mention that her mother had died that year and that going to meetings filled with giggling girls was not something she wanted to do.

Charlie Nugent looked on with bated breath while the lieutenant pondered this information, and after due consideration decided to let it pass.

But he reproached Miri for not having looked at the list first.

The lieutenant next asked whether she was a Communist or had ever belonged to a Communist organization. She said truthfully, no.

Then he asked her if she knew or associated with

any Communists. Her cheeks burned as she again answered no. She hoped it didn't show. After all, one of the other students at Madame Fleuris' pension, Branford Duane Lee the Third, had been a Communist, although Miri didn't know it until Vanessa Tate, who was sleeping with him, told her. She felt guilty about not revealing this tenuous connection, but after all, Vanessa had cooled to her since her painting had become more representational and she had taken the Army job, so they weren't even getting together anymore. And Vanessa had broken off with Bran after meeting a suave Spanish lawyer at *Semana Santa* in Seville.

Upon short reflection, the lieutenant decided to reject her. She heard him tell Mister Jayes that her fluent French was suspect, as was her attempt to avoid looking at the subversive organizations list. (Sometime afterward, Charlie explained to her that there was a U.S. senator named Joseph McCarthy who was driving everyone crazy trying to ferret out Communist-tainted citizens and the witch-hunt even extended to citizens working overseas; maybe especially to them.)

"Surely you and Charlie can find a better clerk-typist who is also an American citizen? The Sorbonne is crawling with them."

But Mr Jayes said calmly, "Charlie has already interviewed fifty-seven preening giggling girls who are dying to stay in Paris now that their third year abroad is about to end. Any one of them would drive Charlie nuts. But this one doesn't preen and she doesn't giggle and Charlie likes her, so Lieutenant, may we please get on with our work? You know Kitty is bitching about the extra work she's had to do. Besides, Private Levin recommended this girl."

"Probably because he was making out with her," the lieutenant grumbled. But he was close to relenting, because Private Levin was the closest thing to a friend he had at FOUSAP.

"'That may be,'" said Mr Jayes calmly, "but as he is a sound young man whose integrity has never been in question, I doubt he would risk censure by recommending anyone who would be an embarassment to the U.S. Army."

After a pause the lieutenant said sternly, "I'll approve this appointment on condition that a memo be placed in Miss Winter's file stating that final approval was granted at the assurance of Craig Jayes, civilian GS-14."

"Consider it done, Lieutenant. It will be Miss Winter's first task to type it up!"

Miri had avoided Lieutenant Morgan as much as she could after that first day. As long as you weren't late, you rarely saw him. In the morning he would wait by the bottom of the staircase to see what time each person arrived. Since most mornings Miri arrived earlier than the lieutenant, this was one criticism she avoided.

Seymour, however, had spoken well of the lieutenant. In the first place, he was a war hero. He got shot up at Anzio trying to protect his men, and had lost a leg below the knee. Furthermore he was "a decent man and an excellent chess-player."

And now the colonel had pronounced what sounded like a sincere eulogy, calling him a "brave man."

She was sorry now that she hadn't liked Lieutenant Morgan better.

Miri had gotten the Army job in late April. It was a big change for her. Before, she had very little money but complete freedom to paint, or go to museums, or sit around in cafes and listen in on intellectual discussions. Or she could rent a tiny chair in the Luxembourg Gardens and spend an afternoon sketching and watching the children rolling hoops, sailing sailboats in the pond, or being trotted around in pony carts led by old men in tatters. Now, for many hours a day, she was restricted to an office, but she had lots of money. If it were just a matter of hedonism she would have preferred the former situation.

But Miri had a goal. She wanted to spend another year in Europe, specifically in Spain. Many

American artists and other foreigners had discovered it and she had heard it was really cheap to live there. Before she took the Army job her savings were running out and she would have had to return to the States and get back into her old routine, working as a waitress or a picker-upper at one of the discount clothing stores where customers trying things on threw on the floor the items they weren't going to buy, and going to the Art Students League, and maybe even squeezing in a course at Columbia's School of General Studies.

Even though she was the second-lowest paid person in FOUSAP (Vic Logan's secretary Marge was the lowest, even though she worked harder than any of the other girls because Vic Logan was a slave-driver), her salary was not only more than sufficient for her needs, she could still save enough after a year to go to Spain to paint.

She had heard from other art students who had been there that you could live on one or two dollars a day. And she was receiving not only a munificent salary, but a rent allowance and a hardship allowance. The latter was for "suffering by being away from home." Miri thought that was very funny, that anyone could be said to suffering hardship by living in Paris instead of Peachtree, Georgia, the Finance Department's headquarters. And of course, they could buy food, clothing, liquor, gasoline and assorted trinkets at the PX for much less money than things cost in French stores.

Judy had wanted Miri to attend her wedding. Her father had agreed to pay all Miri's travelling expenses, as he was doing for Jean-Jacques Pilieu, who was to be Alphie's best man, but Miri turned the offer down. She shuddered at the thought of the gross conspicuous-consumption of the affair, she didn't have anything to wear to such an event and didn't want to buy a fancy dress she would never wear again, and she was terrified of flying. Not attending the wedding turned out to be a fortunate decision because she was then in Paris when Seymour told her about the job at FOUSAP and got her an interview.

By the time Judy Kugel had returned from the States as Madame Alphonse Dantan, Miri had established a tolerable routine, painting for at least two hours after work, and longer on weekends.

Seymour toiled in the basement machine-room. During working hours Seymour was very correct and never mixed business with pleasure, except to go for a quick bite together at lunch time. On Saturday nights though, they were often together, at Seymour's apartment, after a nice meal at a bistro in his neighborhood.

He was uncomfortably affectionate, and his ears stuck out, but since he was really intelligent and well-read, and liked her paintings, that evened things out.

Sometimes they went to a movie. There was a tiny theatre near Cluny that occasionally showed old films. Miri's favorite was *Volpone* with Louis Jouvet, but they only showed it once. They went to see Jean-Louis Philippe in *Le Diable au Corps*. Miri disapproved morally of the married woman's behavior, although that was the whole point of the movie – a devil in the flesh – but she liked the scene where the couple was in a restaurant and with the help of a conspiring waiter, polished off a whole bottle of wine on the pretense of ascertaining if it was corky.

Before the show began the candy-girl would go up and down the aisles with her tray, chanting, "*Bons bons, chocolat, Eskimo Gervais,*" over and over. Seymour would always lean over and buy something from the candy-girl, usually an *Eskimo Gervais,* without asking Miri what she wanted. She probably would have requested an *Eskimo Gervais,* but also would have liked to be asked.

It was nice of Seymour, though, to agree to go to French films even though he didn't speak French. During the picture she tried to whisper translations from the screen during the picture, and that seemed to be enough for him. Of course, he always had his arm around her.

The American films with French subtitles that they showed on the *Boulevard des Capucines* were of no interest to her whatever. That was where her fellow workers went, the only French "culture" they were interested in other than the *Folies Bergere* and the Jockey Club. Maybe it was a hardship for them to be in Paris after all. Maybe they did deserve a "hardship allowance," strange as that seemed. Except for Tony and Harriet, supervisors in the machine-room, who adored the races, and had several beautiful racecourses near Paris to choose from. They went all the time. They had each other, and as they were both somewhat unattractive, this was a gift from heaven. They had the races, and they were blissfully happy.

Miri would have liked to get together with Vanessa Tate at dinner at Reid Hall sometimes during the week, and then look at each other's recent paintings; but Vanessa was no longer interested.

Another blow was that the directress of Reid Hall, Miss Bancroft, let her know that Reid Hall was a residence for American women university students, not clerk-typists. Reid Hall was indeed a residence for American women university students, but as Miri had been one when she moved in, it seemed harsh that it be suggested that she leave once her status changed.

Miri and Miss Bancroft seemed to meet in the halls more frequently than ever, and Miss Bancroft would glare at her and drop broad hints that she had a waiting list of *students.* Miri understood her very well but ignored the hints. She did not want to move out. Her room was a perfect place to paint, and she could take a bath every day without paying extra. But every cold look from Miss Bancroft gave her a nervous feeling.

7

"Any one of dozens of persons in that building could have done it," Chief Inspector Goulette grumbled, glancing dispairingly at the pages listing the personnel which the colonel had provided him. He was sitting with Inspectors Pilieu and Dantan in their usual banquette at the rear of the *Café La Mouche*, near the *Police Judiciare*. "Any one of them could have run up the back stairs and hid in the store-room while they waited for a propitious moment to strike the blow."

Each of the inspectors had his own copy of the personnel list. Dantan went down the list reading each name aloud, the other two men interjecting their few comments picked up from Kitty Hill, who had supplemented the meager data on each of the personnel with her own gossipy comments.

Everyone on the list except Private Levin, who was out-of-town, had been questioned, at least cursorily. Some of them would be questioned again in depth the following day.

The military were listed first:

"Colonel Robert Ritchie. Career military, aged 52, respectable war record, scheduled to retire in less than a year. Not likely to make waves so soon before retirement. Assigned to Paris in 1951.

"Sergeant Carr Southwood, aged 25. Draftee. After training at Fort Bliss in Texas was transferred to Paris. Scion of wealthy steel family. Kitty offered that he was "an arrogant bastard and drives a late-model Cadillac." The latter proved to be unexceptionable: most of the civilians, at least, drove late-model American cars, shipped over courtesy of the U.S. government as part of their personal effects.

"Private Seymour Levin, aged 25. Draftee. Stationed in Garmisch until January 1954, then transferred to Paris. Travels more than a private could be expected to do, between Paris and Garmisch. Reputed to be a nice guy, closed-mouthed, chess pal of the deceased lieutenant.

"Private Peter Parnes, aged 28. Career Army. Enlisted at 20. Nice young guy, undistinguished. Shares an apartment with Charles Nugent. Drives a car owned by Nugent.

"Private Dennis Bernardi, aged 24, Draftee, but might re-enlist. Jovial. Nickname 'Jolly Green Giant'."

Next the civilians:

Sixteen French nationals were on the list. They were not allowed access anywhere in the building except the basement, where they worked. So if they were seen above and hadn't been summoned there, it might be suspicious.

The American civilians consisted of:

"Craig Jayes, aged 42. Senior civilian supervisor. Long-term civilian employe of the Army. A loner who often walks miles and miles around the city.

"Victor Logan, 35. Senior machine-room manager. Long-time civilian employe of the Army. Wife Marianne worked as clerk-typist until March 1954, when she resigned to go Stateside, and was replaced.

"Charles Nugent, 58. Assistant civilian supervisor. Long-term civilian employe of the Army. As mentioned, he and Private Parnes share an apartment." Kitty commented that Charlie had bought the car Peter Parnes drove. "He drives them both to and from work and does all their PX shopping."

"Jacqueline Harris, 27. Files-supervisor. Hired in the States a year ago. A nut for 19th Century German antiques and for the internal combustion engine.

"Carolene Mayce. Keypunching supervisor. Long-term civilian employe of the Army. Sent to Paris as a compassionate act, when her husband, also civilian employe of the Army, died suddenly.

"Harriet Barlow, 39. Verifying supervisor. Career civilian. Sleeping with Tony Alotta but has her own place.

"Tony Alotta, 38. Printing supervisor. Mad about the races.

"William Terk, 36. Printing-operator.

"Barney Porter, 36. Printing-operator.

"Al Rumsey, 37. Printing-operator.

"Eddie Keyser, 28. Printing-operator.

"Marjory Young, aged 29. Clerk-typist to Victor Logan.

"Kitty Hill, aged 27. Secretary to the colonel and the lieutenant.

"Miri Winter, aged 23. Clerk-typist to Messrs Jayes and Nugent. Hired locally in March 1954 after sudden departure of Marianne Logan.

"The victim, Lieutenant John Morgan, aged 32. Wounded at Anzio, lost a leg, decorated for bravery, bronze heart, after a long hospital stay declined retirement and assigned to desk-job, Garmisch, until February 1954, then Paris.

"All personnel had access to the first floor, either by the principal staircase or the back stairs."

"What about cleaning-women?" Goulette asked.

"Kitty Hill told us that a cleaning-woman comes in once a week, from a cleaning-service Mondays."

"Seems very little."

"Security considerations, I guess."

"Assuming everyone else had left, how did the killer get to the lieutenant without arousing his suspicions?" Pilieu asked.

Dantan ventured the opinion that the lieutenant had himself planned a rendezvous with his assailant.

"If it was a meeting the lieutenant requested after work on Friday then there was some reason for having it after hours, when everyone else, including the colonel, had left. The medical examiner said that death probably occurred Friday night or Saturday morning, based on the state of *rigor mortis*. Probably died from a blunt instrument trauma to the skull. The doctor couldn't say where the killing occurred, except that the victim had not died in the spot where he was found. Either his body was moved down the stairs, or, highly unlikely but not totally impossible, he was still alive after being struck and had somehow gotten himself to the stairs, where he tumbled down. A further examination of the body might give clues as to whether the latter was the case."

"But if it was the killer who moved the body, why?"

Dantan shrugged. "If we knew that, we might have a suspect." He planned on interrogating Private Bernardi further. Bernardi, as a big strong fellow could have moved the body with little difficulty.

Pilieu, who had questioned the French staff, had been assured that none of them had gone upstairs for any reason, and all left on time through the basement door, witnessed by Vic Logan.

Dantan had asked Logan if he actually counted the staff members as they exited, to be sure they all had left. Logan had not, but he was sure he would have noticed if someone were missing.

Goulette went over their plans for the next day. He himself would be meeting with Colonel Ritchie again, awaiting the arrival of the American investigating officers. Pilieu was to extend his interviews to the neighbors of all civilians who were managers or supervisors, to try to get observations on their movements the past Friday evening.

They were also awaiting reports on any forensic evidence collected by the technicians, presumably forthcoming the next day.

Goulette bid them a good evening, and left. Pilieu and Dantan remained in the bar, talking companionably. They had been friends since meeting in a military hospital in adjoining cots, recovering from wounds sustained fighting in Indo-China. Pilieu had recovered from his war-wounds first. When Dantan was discharged from the hospital and the army months later, Pilieu had persuaded Goulette to hire his friend, recently out of a military hospital, despondent and without resources, as an English interpreter. This was a great boon to Dantan.

Their friendship became closer. They picked up American girls together in *cafés* fashionable with students, until Dantan fell in love – with an American! – and actually married her! (Sleeping with them, not necessarily marrying them, had been Pilieu's plan.)

"It's not exactly true that anyone could have done it," Pilieu reflected. "Let's agree that the killer and the lieutenant had a planned rendezvous. Let's say that the killer bashed in the lieutenant's skull on the spur of the moment. What would have been lying around handy for the job? There was no convenient fireplace with andirons, tongs.... Nothing. And what if it had been a planned attack? The killer would have brought his weapon with him. But where could he have concealed it until it was needed?"

"He could have hidden a hammer, for example, on his person. It wouldn't have to be very large, as long as it was heavy."

"And took it away when he left."

"Motive, means and opportunity. And the most mysterious of these is motive."

And on that note the two men parted, Pilieu to his solitary apartment near the Pantheon, Dantan home to his sweet little wife and their huge apartment near the Luxembourg Gardens, bought by his father-in-law.

As he strode home Dantan felt anxiety that the P.J. would not be able to solve this case before the Americans took it away from them.

Within three days Colonel Ritchie would surely have met with investigators from the American military, officers of the U.S. Army Criminal Investigation Command from Virginia. The colonel would then invite Chief Inspector Goulette to a meeting of all parties in his office, and inform him, through Armand and an American interpreter, that the U.S. investigators were prepared to take over the investigation. Goulette would have to hand over all forensic evidence the P.J. had gathered, all reports related to it, as well as all statements taken.

Everything had originally been written in French and was in process of being translated for the Americans. But Dantan was almost certain the Americans would want their own translators to do it over. So far Armand was doing the whole job, but Dantan might be required to help if the Americans arrived sooner than expected. Goulette would offer to be of continuing assistance in the investigation even after all the reports were turned over, but the offer was unlikely to be received with enthusiasm.

Dantan was frustrated not to be able to see the case through. He wasn't sure he would have succeeded at solving it, but he would not even have much opportunity to try.

He had become the *de facto* leader of the investigation because of his command of English. When Dantan had voiced his frustration to his chief, Goulette assured him that there was nothing to stop him from pursuing his own ideas, as long as the Americans did not get the impression he was impeding them, or trying to take over. "Discretion" was the watchword. Chief Inspector Goulette was not going to impede Dantan in whatever he wanted to do as long as he didn't incur criticism from the Americans, or stir up feelings of animosity.

8

Miri painted for over an hour, but had a heavy heart and stopped earlier than she would have liked. She would go early to the Dantans. It was an enjoyable walk across the Luxembourg Gardens to their apartment. She would have picked up a bottle of wine to bring over except that she knew nothing about wine and didn't care to learn, she never touched the stuff; so she settled for a colorful nosegay from a flower vendor on the *Boul' Mich'*.

Judy drew Miri into the nearer salon. (The farther salon had no furniture yet, and there was no rush as they had no use for it.) There were a couple of comfortable easy chairs upholstered in maroon plush, but two of the walls were still in need of plaster and paint.

"One of these days the work will be finished," Judy sighed.

"It's going to be magnificent," Miri said politely, although she couldn't imagine what two people would do with all that space. Two salons, large dining-room, four bedrooms! Plus two *chambres de bonnes* under the roof. Germaine occupied one of these small servants' rooms. In the other, Judy had stored her winter clothes. Even if Judy and Alphonse decided to add a drooling blob to the world's population, thought Miri, that still left two empty bedrooms. Her parents probably wouldn't want to stay there, they were too accustomed to the *haute* luxury of the *Palais Royale*.

Judy led Miri through a small doorway to take a peek at the handsome den she had had carved for Alphie out of a corner of the salon, giving him the high fireplace with an impressive green marble mantel. "My mother thought I should have kept the fireplace in the salon and put Alphie's den in one of the extra bedrooms, but he only wanted a small space and the fireplace made it cosy."

They returned to the salon, and sank into the deep upholstered chairs.

"I wonder if I'll still be here by the time it's all done," Judy said sadly. "If you really want to know, I'm sick and tired of being married to Alphie."

"What!" This was a bombshell Miri could hardly absorb.

"I'm bored with Paris and I'm sick of going shopping. I'm bored with Alphie and all his goofy French *copains*.. He doesn't bathe enough, just takes sponge baths which aren't good enough in July, he won't use the hand-shower we temporarily put in over the kitchen sink, I'm tired of trying to cook French food and I hate the *Cordon Bleu* he's making me go to. The instructor is nasty, I think he hates Americans, and he uses too much butter. And I don't like the kind of clothes Alphie thinks are chic. He wants me to get rid of my most favorite shoes and sweaters. I don't enjoy shopping anymore, I don't like having to go back and forth for fittings instead of finding something nice off a rack..."

"What about *prêt à porter?*"

"Junk."

Miri was exasperated with her. "Alphie loves you, and he is a sweet smart handsome sexy man, and you've only been married three months! You're spoiled is what you are. You're bored with yourself. You have nothing on your mind, so everything bores you."

"I know," Judy wailed. "But I don't know what to do! I miss my friends at home."

"Well have them come and visit and stay with you for awhile. They can afford the passage. But I have a better idea than hanging out with a bunch of spoiled empty-headed girls from Great Neck – go back to school! Get a real degree in something real. Quit that stupid *Cordon Bleu* and stop drinking wine every evening, that's what's probably making you morose. I never touch the stuff and I'm much more cheerful than you." In truth, Miri was not a cheerful person, nor did she want to be thought of as one, but saying that seemed a way to pull Judy out of the doldrums.

"You always think some kind of intellectual activity is the solution. Well it isn't."

"Well for goodness' sake don't say anything about this to Alphie. Suppose it's just a passing bad mood? He deserves better treatment than that. And don't breathe a word to your parents. Think about how you felt when you fell in love with him. I saw you two, you weren't able to keep your hands off each other."

"You're not particularly nice to Seymour."

"In the first place, I'm not married to him. In the second place, I didn't pull any melodramatic acts on my parents to get them to come around to the idea of a marriage they didn't want to happen, or make them want to spend a fortune on an obscenely conspicuous-consumption wedding, and lavish you with a lot of stuff besides, to say nothing of this apartment and about a million dollars worth of improvements. And thirdly, I'm not that mean to Seymour, I just get confused sometimes about how I feel about him."

By this time Judy was weeping into a hand-embroidered linen handkerchief, carefully laundered and ironed by Germaine.

Miri didn't particularly want a closer friendship with Judy than they had already, because she thought Judy was shallow and this only proved it. Nevertheless, she felt an impulse to help her, to help her give up these thoughts and feel good about being with Alphie. And she felt sorry for Alphie, who could easily have become a typical Frenchman, having affairs, and taking his wife's money, like Monsieur Fleuris at the *pension*, but hadn't done so. Also, Miri had had a crush on Alphonse Dantan before she found out about him and Judy, and thought he was very nice.

"You might solve the bath thing by showering together in that crowded little space. Soap each other up and fool around. Just don't fall out of the sink from laughing!"

Judy giggled. "Do you do that with Seymour?"

Miri ignored this. "Want me to help you search out some good courses at the Sorbonne?"

"No. But you're right about one thing. I'm going to quit that darn *Cordon Bleu*."

"Wait! I just got another idea for you besides going to the Sorbonne. There's that woman in FOUSAP who collects antique furniture. She's not just buying old stuff, she's reading up on it in German. She had to learn the language so she could read those old tomes on the subject she finds when she goes to Germany. That's a real collector for you.

"Your father has enough money for you to become a collector of something. Once you decide what, that would give you something to study up on, and the shopping would be much more interesting than buying more sweaters and skirts. You've got lots of storage space in this apartment and you're in Paris where there's lots of old stuff to buy cheap. All sorts of things. Rare old books, Sevres vases, antique furniture...."

"Too rickety and scratched and usually uncomfortable. My mother spends hours and hours trying to get restorers to do things right."

If Judy didn't want to collect old furniture, Miri had other ideas.

"There's all kinds of stuff at the *Marché aux Puces*. Crystal, antique jewelry, though I personally think if you have more jewelry than you can wear at one time you have too much. All I have is the garnet earrings Seymour bought for me at the PX and I don't feel the need for anything more.

"What about paintings? If you wanted to buy anything from unknown art students I could tell you which ones were good and which ones weren't." Miri wasn't sure yet if she would be able to swallow her pride and contact Vanessa Tate, whose work was quite good.

Judy, who loved to shop and was not stupid, only vacuous, immediately liked the idea. "Paintings! I already have the one you gave me, and you can help me discover new talent. And of course I would buy Old Masters if I could find any. There are lots of walls to cover here. My mother wanted me to buy big antique tapestries for the salons and dining room but I think paintings will be better. Maybe I could make the second salon into a sort of art gallery, just paintings, no furniture. That would save schlepping around for furniture I don't even need."

"Well just keep your mother out of your art selections."

"I know. She knows *bubkes*."

They both giggled, remembering the same incident, before the wedding, when Mrs Kugel had come to Paris with her daughter for a week to do some shopping for gifts for bridesmaids and ushers.

Judy had dropped in on Miri at Reid Hall on their Saturday in Paris. "My mother insisted on coming along, 'just to say hello to Miri', she's huffing and puffing her way up the stairs now," Judy warned her. Judy suspected that her mother still didn't trust Miri not to subvert her daughter in some way, even though it was basically too late, she was marrying her daughter off to a man who was not an American, not a Jew, not a professional man.

Judy planned to shake her mother by escorting her to a wonderful leather-goods shop on *Boulevard Montparnasse*, where she could spend hours selecting gifts for the ushers, then adjourn to the shop next door, which carried dazzling silk scarves.

Miri had been painting, wearing paint-smeared jeans and a gray sweatshirt, an outfit she had copied from Vanessa Tate. She had turned some of her new paintings outward, ones she had done working from the old Maisel photographs, and she had also displayed her portrait of Bethel Washton in the Chinese robe. Her plan was to see how Judy reacted to it, and then decide whether or not to give it to her as a wedding present.

Mrs Kugel arrived upstairs winded and was immediately put off by Miri's appearance. She had hoped to take the girls to someplace nice for tea. Judy and Miri smirked at each other.

The two visitors looked at each painting thoughtfully, Mrs Kugel, with lips pursed. At the painting of Bethel Washton she stopped. "Is that a *Negress*?" she shrieked.

Miri said coolly, "She happens to be a terrific actress who is going to be a big star in Hollywood. But mainly I painted her because of her bone structure and regal bearing."

"Well I think it's ugly!" Mrs Kugel declared.

Judy said nothing. It was obvious to Miri that

if she gave the painting to the newlyweds and if they liked it, it still wouldn't be hung in their new home because of Mrs Kugel.

"Whatever happened to that boyfriend you had back in the winter?" Mrs Kugel demanded.

"He's out-of-town right now."

"So is anything going to come of it?"

"Oh Mommy don't be so nosey! When Miri gets engaged I'm sure she'll tell me and I'll be sure to tell you. Tell you what. Let's go shopping and let Miri get some more work done." She winked at Miri behind her mother's back.

"You call that 'work'?" Mrs Kugel huffed. But she went off with Judy.

A short time later, having deposited her mother at the leather-goods shop, she returned to Reid Hall. Miri had changed into a black skirt and the red cashmere sweater Judy had foisted on her during the winter at the *pension* and was ready to go to a *café* and talk.

"Your mother didn't like my painting of Bethel Washton."

"I hope your idea of an art critic is not my mother! She knows *bubkes*."

"Are you kidding? It's just that I was thinking of giving you that painting as a wedding gift. But now I can't. She'll keep on saying nasty things every time she sees it, and might even throw it away."

"I'd rather have the one of the little girl in the lacy dress," Judy said wistfully. This painting of an angelic-looking five-year old was based on an old photograph Miri had found among the efects of the Maisel family.

Miri was thrilled that Judy had actually looked at her paintings closely enough to like one! It put her on the verge of tears. "Okay," she said gruffly.

"You're coming to the wedding, right? Remember, I telegraphed you that my Daddy is going to pay your fare, round-trip, so you can attend."

"I can't let him do that. It isn't right."

"What's wrong with it? He has money, you don't, I want you at my wedding, so it's like a present to me if he makes it possible for you to attend."

"No. I'm not taking his money, and I'm afraid of flying, and I can't spare the time to go back and forth by boat." Miri also assumed nobody there would like her, but didn't mention this. "You can take the painting with you when you go home this time."

Judy planted a big kiss on Miri's cheek.

"Ugh!" said Miri. "I'm not big on kissing."

"Well I am. But I've got lots of other people to kiss, so it's okay," Judy giggled.

The next day, Miri had taken the painting of the little girl in the lacy dress to Judy at the *Palais Royale*.

"Will you teach me what I need to know about art?" Judy asked plaintively.

Miri shook her head. "I need to learn a lot myself. But I could help you choose books. And we could go look at things in museums. I saw an exhibit at the Modern Art Museum of an artist I think is really exciting. Georges Rouault. It was a temporary exhibition. Wonderful. Someday his paintings will be worth a lot more, after he's dead. Try to get your daddy to buy you a Rouault. He may not like Rouault's work because he sometimes paints Christ, but he also paints clowns so maybe that evens things out."

Judy was returning to her own bubbly self already. She loved the idea.

Miri couldn't believe she was committing herself in this way, but if she could get an empty-headed rich girl interested in collecting real art it would be real service to the art world. And maybe Judy would even become less empty-headed.

The telephone rang on a little gilded French table next to the main sofa and Judy dashed to it. "That's my Mommy!"

To give her privacy, Miri wandered into the huge old kitchen to say hello to Germaine. Germaine's wrinkled face crinkled into a smile. Miri sat on a little kitchen chair while Germaine pounded away with a masher at a big bowl of potatoes, adding liberal amounts of cream and butter and salt and pepper. She checked on the roast in the coal oven. She shoveled more coals from a bucket on the floor into the glowing pit of the stove. Miri savored the charcoal aroma. The raw string beans were on a wooden table awaiting cutting. Miri offered to help but Germaine was horrified at the thought, either because Miri was a young lady and therefore shouldn't do this kind of work, or because Germaine thought she would be incompetent to slice them just right.

As she worked, Germaine brought Miri up-to-date on the doings of their old acquaintances from the *pension* Fleuris. Somehow, Miri, who considered gossip beneath her, enjoyed it when it was in French.

Gabrielle was still working with the American family in their big house in *Saint-Germain-en-Laye*, and had fallen in love with one of the young men of the family. Germaine prayed for her every week that she would not become *enceinte*.

Monsieur Fleuris and his mistress were still happy together, she was doing a good business with her millinery and he with his baking. He had added *baguettes* to his *palmiers*. They were wonderful. Germaine always fetched some for the Dantans' Sunday breakfast.

Germaine had seen the gentlemanly *Monsieur* Jamie Giardini at Eastertime. He had brought her a big bunch of flowers.

She had heard that Madame Poivriere's son and his wife had had a baby.

At some point, it was inevitable that Germaine would learn about the murder among the Americans since her master was investigating it. Miri told her enough about it to send a little shiver through the old servant.

9

Miri had not been to dinner at the Dantans since May. This was not for want of invitations from Judy. Miri was still trying to keep her friendships exclusively to those she considered serious artists and thinkers; therefore she had almost none.

Earlier that month, Miri had received a *pneumatique* from Renee Rubin, with whom she had lost touch. Renee was a deadly-serious philosophy student in Paris on a Fulbright scholarship. Miri had met her at the American Club for Students and Artists back when Miri was studying at the *Ecole des Beaux Arts* and living at the *pension* Fleuris. She had been impressed and also intimidated by Renee's intense intellectualism, but as this was precisely the kind of person Miri felt she ought to be associating with, she made every effort to keep up with Renee.

After the murder at the *pension* on *Rue des Ecoles* a storeroom there was found to contain papers and possessions of the Maisels, a Jewish family who had lived there during the war before they had been denounced and sent to the Nazi death-camps. Renee had pounced on the family documents and had begun writing a book about the Maisel family in the context of how the French had treated French Jews during the war. Miri had also made use of materials from the storeroom, principally old photographs of members of the family, as a basis for paintings that would reflect their innocent lives compared to their deaths.

After that discovery in January, the two girls had lost touch. Now Renee was sending her the message, "Please telephone me immediately. It's very urgent.— Renee." She gave a number. "In case you can't reach me by phone, send me a *pneu* at the following address. I've moved." She gave an address which Miri found, after looking it up in her *Plan de Paris*, was in *Le Marais*.

Miri wondered who it was urgent for, but she did call the number, and she heard Renee's husky voice at the other end.

Before she got to the urgent matter, Renee complained that she had tried to telephone Miri at Reid Hall but the operator would not call her to the phone.

"They wouldn't. You have to leave a message."

Renee did not know about Miri's new job. She assumed that Miri was still studying at the *Ecole des Beaux*

Arts. "I need you to do something for me at your school."
She wanted Miri to search out young men with a certain
background. Renee had gotten as far with her book about
the Maisels as she could, and had decided to broaden its
scope to write about other Jewish families in France during the war. She had already gotten additional grant
money to continue working on the book and could stay
in Paris another year if she wanted.

Renee wanted Miri to locate Frenchmen who had
been living in Paris during the Occupation or elsewhere
in Vichy France, young people who had been children
or youths then. She wanted to hear their experiences. If
they had known any Jews, so much the better. "My guess
is that if they were only kids during the war they will
speak more freely than anyone who was an adult at that
time, and possibly has something to hide. To hear them
talk they were all in the Resistance, but if there really
were that many men and women in the Resistance, France
could have thrown the Germans out with ease."

So this was the "urgent" matter!

"I'm not at the *Beaux Arts* anymore. I have a full-
time job." After Vanessa Tate's negative reaction, Miri
was loathe to mention that she working at a U.S. Army
office. In finance, no less. That would really inspire the
scorn of a philosopher.

"Well, don't you still know anyone at the *Beaux
Arts*?"

"I haven't really stayed in touch. Didn't you stay in

touch with anyone from the *Cité Universitaire*? You lived there long enough."

"Nobody French. Students come from all over the world to stay there, and I was more involved with people of other nationalities."

Miri was inclined to refuse Renee's request. Renee was bossy, and Miri, despite her admiration for her intellectual capacity, felt intimidated by it.

"I've gotten in with a crowd of American intellectuals," Renee said, "and that is not an oxymoron!"

Miri took her word for that, as she had no idea what an oxymoron was.

"They have gotten together to start a literary periodical which will be devoted to works-in-progress by Americans living abroad. Such as the members of this group. I'm hoping that they'll read my work-in-progress and print an exerpt."

"What's the magazine called?"

"They don't have a name for it yet. They're still wrangling over who will be the senior editor. The guy whose father is funding the magazine wants to be in charge, but so far some others are trying on the grounds of having more degrees from fancier universities, like Oxford. But I believe it's really going to happen. They're all brilliant."

Miri thought it would be interesting to meet these "brilliant intellectual" Americans. So she reconsidered Renee's request. It was true that she hadn't kept in touch with any of the students from the *Beaux Arts*; but she could put Judy to work on the problem! Judy loved matchmaking. This wasn't exactly matchmaking but then again you never knew. Of course Renee had not liked Judy when she met her at the pension, in fact had referred to her more than once as "*la vache qui rit*" (the laughing cow, a brand of cheese). But she might not refuse a favor from her anyway.

"I'll try. I can't promise anything."

Renee said thank you and hung up.

Judy had been leaving messages at Reid Hall for Miri, invitations to dinner "at our new apartment even though it is still a mess" but Miri hadn't responded. Now she telephoned Judy that very evening and was greeted enthusiastically.

"Does Jean-Jacques Pilieu have a girlfriend yet?" Miri asked.

"Why? Are you interested in the role?" Judy giggled.

"Are you kidding? He's not my type at all. He looks goofy. This is about something else." She told Judy of Renee Rubin's request to meet young Frenchmen who had been kids in Paris during the German Occupation so that she could pick their brain for her book. "She would probably go to bed with them if she has to."

"I don't know if that's such an inducement. Renee looks like a duck."

"Just what I think too!" Miri laughed. "But it might not matter. Jean-Jacques always seems to be...

you know...."

"Horny!"

Both girls giggled. Miri refrained from remarking that Seymour was horny, too.

"Who knows? It might work," Judy said more soberly. "And Jean-Jacques could work on his English. Which is still atrocious."

"And Renee could improve her French. They could be each other's sleeping dictionary!"

Both girls broke into peals of laughter.

"I'll tell Alphie about it and ask him to invite Jean-Jacques."

Alphie agreed to do so provided it was on a weekend in case he and Jean-Jacques had to work long and late on an investigation. He only wished. Since Dantan had been promoted to Inspector, there had been no serious or interesting cases; that is, murders.

The more Judy thought about it the more perfect it seemed. Jean-Jacques was unattached, had grown up in Paris, really liked foreign girls, and was a good friend of Alphie's.

Judy was happy to be planning a party again, just like she had done in Great Neck before she was married, even if it were going to be only the five of them. It would be nice if there were even more people coming. Maybe Alphie could think of someone who spoke both French and English, even if he had not lived under the Occupation as a boy.

What about Armand! The boyish interpreter at the P.J. who had replaced Alphie in that position when Alphie was promoted to Inspector.

But if Miri's boyfriend Seymour were in town, he should be invited too, and then she should try to invite another girl to make it even.

"Do you think you could find a suitable girl at Reid Hall, so we can round it up to eight?" she asked Miri.

Miri immediately thought of the two singers on Fulbrights, Felice, the little dark-haired contralto, and Liddy, the statuesque blonde soprano. They had always been friendly to Miri, although they never got together except at meals. Liddy had confided to Miri that they both would like to meet American men; they only seemed to meet foreigners or homosexuals as they made their rounds from classes to tutoring to language lessons to performances to concerts.

Both singers were incipient linguists. They were learning German, Spanish, Italian and French because they had to sing in so many languages. This made them invaluable for communicating with Armand and Jean-Jacques in French.

The two singers seemed to do everything together — taking lessons with Nadia Boulanger, attending the same concerts. The little dark one, Felice, had a fiery temper, which was useful in performing Carmen but less so in getting along with directors and other people. She had been trying to get a job with one of the small opera

companies to be found all over Germany, but had had no
luck so far. Liddy, the phlegmatic blonde was sticking to
lieder and arias; she could make money singing in concerts and churches, and it got her name around.

Miri decided she could not invite one without the
other, and at the next Reid Hall meal went ahead and
issued invitations to them both, no date yet, for Judy
Dantan's dinner party. "Her husband is an inspector with
the *Police Judiciare*."

Both singers pronounced this thrilling and were delighted to accept. With identical silver pencils they each
wrote the possible dates for Judy's party into their little
crammed calf-covered datebooks.

Then Miri heard from Seymour. He was coming to
Paris, and bringing his friend from Garmisch, Private Nate
Roth, who would be staying at his apartment for a few
days. Nate was mad about opera, so Seymour requested
that Miri pick up tickets for the three of them, preferably
a Verdi or Puccini, but knowing the French chauvinism
thought they would have to settle for *Pelleas et Melisande*
or *Faust*. Miri thought this boded well for Nate's meeting with two opera singers at Judy's party!

The days that Seymour and Nate would be in Paris
were satisfactory to Judy, and she began issuing invitations for Saturday night.

Miri got the idea of having her own little dinner-
party of sorts, at Reid Hall. She would invite Seymour
and Nate and sit them together with the two singers.

Then Miri began to worry that there were the two girls, and she only wanted them to meet Nate, not get interested in Seymour. She hit upon the idea of inviting both singers, Seymour and Nate, and a third man, too. She would invite Dennis Bernardi. Her plan was to have all three men as her guests at dinner at Reid Hall, a very cheap way to entertain, and the six of them could take almost a whole table. Felice and Liddy and Dennis loved the idea, and Seymour always agreed to anything Miri wanted. Judy hearing this plan then invited Dennis to her own party, too.

Miri made arrangements with the Reid Hall cook for three extra persons. Felice and Liddy promised to get to the dining-room early enough to stake a claim to a whole table, Seymour, Nate and Dennis Bernardi showed up together, expecting to have a very good time.

And they did -- up to a point. Nate was taken with both singers, who promised to sing for him if they could find a spot that wouldn't disturb anyone. (A man was not allowed into any of the girls' rooms unless he was a doctor making an emergency call, or a priest there to administer last rites if the doctor failed at his task.)

Much to Miri's dismay, Seymour seemed especially struck by the fiery little contralto. Even Dennis, who everyone knew was obsessed with Jackie Harris at the office, showed vivid interest in Felice too.

Later, when Miss Bancroft learned that Miss Winter had invited *three* men to dinner she was livid. In her eyes Miri was a harlot. Added to this, Miss Bancroft felt that Miri did not belong at Reid Hall because she was no longer a student, but a working-girl, a clerk-typist, Miss Bancroft informed Miss Winter that she was to leave Reid Hall as swiftly as possible.

Felice and Liddy were sympathetic (especially since by then Liddy had made a date with Nate) and offered to plead her case with Miss Bancroft, but Miri declined their kind offer. She didn't think it would work. She felt that Miss Bancroft would be implacable, and she didn't want to be humiliated when the plea was denied.

The next evening, Saturday, was Judy Dantan's dinner-party. Miri was feeling terrible anxiety about where she was going to live. She had no idea of how to look for a place, now that she was no longer a student with student housing services accessible to her. Besides, she loved living at Reid Halll and didn't want to leave. She wouldn't tell Seymour; she was too proud.

Seymour, Nate and Dennis picked her up in a taxi.

"You're so quiet," Dennis joshed her. "Cat got your tongue?"

"I'm okay," she said. But she went to Judy's party with a heavy heart.

At the Dantans' apartment, still in extreme disrepair from the renovations going on, the guests were shown into a large elegant dining-room furnished with the mahogany table, chairs, sideboard and silver-chest the Dantan had purchased from Jean-Jacques' mother. He smiled at the sight of them.

Armand was in awe of the Dantans' apartment. He was quite shy about speaking with anyone until Renee got his ear and made conversation easy for him as he never got a chance to utter a word. Judy had seated Renee between Armand and Jean-Jacques for maximum opportunity to pursue her topic. Armand's English was excellent, though heavily accented.

Renee launched into a description of her new apartment. She had been living at the *Cité Universitaire* since her arrival in Paris, and had met many interesting students from other countries, but felt now it was time to get her own place and soak up some authentic atmosphere that would help her with her book. She had moved into an apartment in the Jewish quarter of *Le Marais*.

Miri remembered nostalgically her visits to the *Place des Vosges* with Jamie Guardini; one time they had looked at it by moonlight, another time they went in the daytime and had visited the *Musée Carnavalet* and admired *Hotel de Sully* which was slated to be restored. But she had never seen the Jewish Quarter, nor did it interest her.

"How did you go about finding an apartment?" Miri asked. "I need one too. They're kicking me out of Reid Hall."

"What!" Judy shrieked. "They can't do that."

"Miss Bancroft says the place is for American women students. And I'm not a student anymore."

Seymour expressed serious concern. He immediately suggested she move in with him. But he wanted to hear all the details. He knew a couple of guys in the Judge Adjutant General's and maybe they could think of some legal way to insist that Reid Hall keep her there. "But in the meantime you have a home with me. Now tell me what happened."

Miri omitted mentioning the part that having three men to dinner had played in Miss Bancroft's edict. She mentioned only that Reid Hall was deemed for American university women and Miri was now a full-time clerk-typist.

"She's a bitch," Felice remarked.

"A mean bitch," Liddy agreed.

Renee said, "You could move in with me. I've got lots of space and you could help out a lot when I have the brilliant intellectual Americans over. You could pass around snacks and wine so I won't have to interrupt conversations with any of them to do the serving. And you can help me practice my French. And buy stuff for us at the PX, things like Kotex and toilet paper. That would be a big saving."

Judy and Miri smiled embarassedly at each other at the mention of Kotex, but nobody else seemed to have noticed.

The thought of living in the old Jewish quarter, dilapidated and swarming with religious old people in black did not appeal to her, nor did living with Renee Rubin, who talked too much, was too bossy, and just wanted her there to come in handy and to tutor her in spoken French. Renee read French fluently, but she talked so much and she never listened to anyone else, therefore had not yet accustomed her ear to the other language.

On the other hand Miri had no idea how to find an apartment, and hated the idea of bothering. It was a dilemma.

"That's very nice of you," Miri said, horrified at the thought of such close proximity to Renee and no escape from her incessant discourse, "but I need space to paint."

"But I have plenty of space. Extra rooms, though not much furniture. You could have two rooms, one to paint in."

"Take it!" Judy cried. "It sounds wonderful!"

Even Seymour was encouraging. It certainly solved her problem even if it was going to create new ones, which usually happened when you took the easy way.

"That's settled then." As far as Renee was concerned the debate was over.

Renee was quite thrilled to have moved into the dilapidated Jewish Quarter of *Le Marais*, describing the little shops, many of them selling one kind of Middle European Jewish food or another, the religious women shuffling along muffled up in shawls, the old Jewish men who had returned after the war after being hidden by Christians, sometimes even elsewhere in France.

Her own landlord was originally from middle Europe, had become a French citizen before the war but when the French government began requiring Jews to wear yellow stars and forbade them certain public facilities, he ran from France to Spain while one still could. After the war he came back to Paris to reclaim the real estate he had bought in safer times.

He now made his livelihood by renting out two apartments (one of them to Renee) which he had managed to get back from the Frenchman who had been the *administrateur provisoire* of his and other properties of Jewish owners when they were deported. He also changed money on the black market in one of the *cafés* near *Châtelet.* There were always merchants who wanted American dollars and were willing to pay a premium for them to avoid filing forms with the bureaucrats, and there were always American students with American dollar traveller checks.

Judy and Miri smiled knowingly at each other; they had changed travellers checks in a *café* with just such an old man from somewhere, not France, and had drunk hot tea in a glass with him while he did his calculations.

Renee got along very well in the neighborhood. She loved the atmosphere. She was sure she could meet people who would give her material for her book, and as she spoke Yiddish fluently, she didn't have to worry about struggling in French with people who could barely speak it themselves.

Miri couldn't have been more comfortable at Reid Hall, where she could have a bath every day, had a room

large enough for her painting, and had a balcony over-
looking a pretty garden. The idea of moving into a crumbling neighborhood that probably smelled strongly of
repellent cooking, and living with Renee, who would
never stop talking, and bossing her around, was unap-
pealing. But moving in with Seymour was not right, even
though they were passing passionate nights in his oversized American bed. And she had no other ideas on how
to find housing.

Renee offered an open invitation to any or all at the
table to come visit, and get a tour of the neighborhood.
They could always go to the *Place des Vosges* afterwards
to see one of the most beautiful spots in Paris.

"That sounds like fun," Felice said.

Liddy agreed.

"We're going to take you up on it."

Miri was surprised.

Dantan asked each of the three soldiers what they
did in the Army.

"I help with the archival files in the Paris office,"
Dennis shrugged. "Not very exciting, but the files manager is cute."

Nate said that he worked in Ordnance in Garmisch
-- he didn't explain because the men knew what Ordnance was and the girls didn't care -- and Seymour said
he helped with the automatic data processing in the Paris
office. None of the three men seemed eager to elaborate.

Dantan asked Seymour, "Don't you travel a lot between Garmisch and Paris? I thought Judy told me that."

Seymour said that this was so.

"Isn't that unusual, for a private?"

"Unusual. But not unheard of."

As he was not in his role as an inspector, but as a host, Dantan did not press his questions. But he did think Seymour was uncommonly closed-mouthed.

Miri was seated next to Jean-Jacques, with Seymour on her right, while the hot-tempered contralto, Felice, was on Seymour's left. She seemed very taken with him. This did not escape Miri's notice, and she suddenly felt threatened at losing her boyfriend and made a resolution to be nicer to him in future.

Before dessert, Judy asked the two singers if they would perform for them.

Each sang *a cappella*. Felice gave them a fiery rendition of an aria from *Carmen*; Seymour applauded enthusiastically, as did the others. Liddy sang *Exultate Jubilate* like an angel. It astonished Miri once again how religion, so full of myths, lies, and fairy tales, could have inspired so much incredible art, music, and architecture through the centuries.

Judy managed to turn the conversation to the subject, after all, that they were there for: to help Renee collect material for her book on the Jews in France during the war.

Alphie had nothing to contribute. An orphan, he had been shipped to the relative safety of England early in the war by his sole living relative, an elderly great-aunt. She could not afford to feed her grand-nephew and could not cope with a twelve-year's natural rambunctiousness. With the aid of her priest (the *cure* had a connection to the Underground) she had managed to have Alphonse included with a group of Jewish children being smuggled out of France. And so, late one chilly night, the boy was wrapped in tarps and hidden, with several other freezing children, on a fishing-boat sailing for England. Once there, the youngsters were sent to farms in the English countryside, where, along with British children escaping the London Blitz, they were all cared for, fed, schooled, and expected to do their share of chores and farmwork. Alphonse was sixteen when he was finally repatriated to France after the war.

Armand had been a small boy when the war began for the French in June 1940, and ended a few weeks later when the French surrendered and accepted German domination. His family lived in the south of France, where the Vichy government prevailed, so he had not lived under the German Occupation. His family knew one young man about twenty who was Jewish, but had obtained a false identity and passed for a Christian, working on a farm.

Jean-Jacques Pilieu had been thirteen in 1940, and going to a *lycée* in Paris. He was pained at first to recall life inder the Occupation when he was a boy, but soon warmed to his topic and the rapt attention all were giving him.

To make a little money Jean-Jacques had driven a bicycle-taxi most days after school, and every Saturday. Business was pretty good, he charged much less than a regular taxi, who had to pay for scarce petrol.

He made out very well once he got a regular passenger for Saturdays, a middled-aged woman who went faithfully once a week to visit her aged mother in the countryside in a nearby *département*. He peddled his legs into stone to get her there, then waited around for her for a couple hours. Her mother's cook always stuffed him with fresh bread she had baked herself, and milk she had milked herself, and cheese she had made herself. Then she would tuck an extra cheese into his coat for his mother. By the time he drove his customer back to her home in Passy he was feeling good.

His customer was a stout woman, but she was always stouter when she returned than when she left. For under her coat, too, were cheeses and butter and a chicken or two, freshly killed. He discovered this when one of the chickens fell out of her coat and she laughed off her plunder. After that she would sometimes give him a chicken as well as the cheese.

Jean-Jacques' mother gratefully accepted these gifts as food was very scarce in their household. She refused to shop on the black market, as some of her friends did, and she was angry when Jean-Jacques had anything to do with the black market at the *lycee*. She was a God-

fearing woman and thought that the black market was
wrong. Jean-Jacques enjoyed it; it was fun. Instead, his
mother would stand on lines, all day every day, to buy
whatever was available. A piece of fish, perhaps; eggs
rarely; whatever was for sale. She would barter with the
other women, if they had something she wanted and she
had something they wanted. In fact she had never enjoyed herself so much in her life! She got to gossip with
the other women on line, talk over everyone's business
— at least those absent from the line — whose son had
gotten arrested, whose daughter had gone astray with a
German soldier. It was entertainment that exceeded the
fare at the theaters, and it was free.

When the Germans began requiring the Jews to wear
yellow stars of David sewn to their clothing and marked
"Juif" many students showed their outrage by mocking
the practice, wearing yellow stars themselves, sometimes
made of paper, marked "Papuan" or "Goi." Jean-Jacques
had wanted to wear one marked "Goi," but his mother
wouldn't let him. She knew an older woman who had
worn a yellow star embroidered with a cross on her dress,
and she had been arrested.

The yellow stars were just the beginning of ever-
increasing persecution of the Jews, their being barred
from restaurants, theaters, any place of culture or recre-
ation. It ended in mass deportations to the death-camps.

Pilieu told them about a plaque that had been put up
after the Liberation in front of the *Vélodrome de Paris*,

where a mass round-up of French Jews, and Jewish immigrants to France, had been herded. It recalled the thirty thousand Jews who were deported from there to Germany and the extermination camps. Jean-Jacques remembered the last line of the plaque: "YOU ARE FREE! DO NOT FORGET!"

Renee made a note to go look at the plaque, and take a photograph.

But she was having a hard time taking notes; she still hadn't improved her listening French because she wasn't used to listening to anyone. Miri and Judy assured her they would help her fill in the missing pieces.

The two singers had to leave early. They were singing in a church the next morning, not in the choir but as soloists. They thanked Judy, said they had enjoyed themselves immensely, took Renee's address and said they would send her a *pneu* when they could visit, and departed right after the cheese and fruit. After they left, all the men spoke of them enthusiastically. Miri was not unhappy to see them go, especially Carmen.

10

It was a pleasant evening, not overly warm and the sky still with some faint light, when Dantan arrived at the apartment on *Rue de Medicis*. He was looking forward to an aperitif with Judy on their tiny balcony, followed by the *coq au vin* Judy had learned to make more than passably well, no doubt with the assistance of the redoubtable Germaine, and the shiny new German range, imported from America, (America having imported it from Germany), its wiring changed to work in France. Mister Kugel was sparing no expense for his baby.

Dantan would valiantly put up with the American mess that Judy insisted accompany most dinners, fit food only for infants and the toothless senile – so-called "mashed" potatoes. Then he would make a quiet retreat to the small room which Judy had insisted be constructed during the general renovations, and which she called his "den," as if he were some feral creature run to earth....

But he had gotten to love that room. It had been made by taking a slice off the salon at the long end where a green marble fireplace predominated. Judy was not proprietary about the fireplace, disdaining it as a source of heat, and dismissing it as a source of dust, and was perfectly satisfied that it be a fixture in his den. Her mother expressed regret that such a showy thing was to be cut off from their salon, but Judy had overruled her. It was an interesting development of their marriage that Judy had begun to stand up to her parents. Of course, demanding their approval to marry him had certainly been courageous. And from winning that round she took courage from this first success.

Judy had furnished his den with a large cubbyholed oak desk, and oak accountant's chair which spun around, a reading lamp, and a big fat American "recliner" upholstered in maroon plush, like the seats, he thought, in a movie theatre. It looked gross, but was, he had to admit, exquisitely comfortable. It had an attached foot-rest which could be popped up or down with a lever. It had been the first piece of furniture to arrive from America after they came back to Paris following their wedding, and they had

spent many evenings cuddling in it before retiring
to their ample featherbed, which had come from
Switzerland and had arrived by the time they needed
it.

Judy was in the salon, on the telephone, probably with her mother, and the murmur of her voice
through the new wall, which was thin, punctuated
by an occasional giggle, was pleasant. The Kugels
were spending many hundreds of thousands of francs
for these frequent transatlantic telephone calls to
Judy, none of them short, but they seemed to be
able to afford it, and it made Judy happy. Pilieu had
suggested to Dantan that maybe they were talking
treason, trying to draw Judy away from him and back
to the States, but Dantan could not believe that. Not
that they weren't capable of it. But his sweeet little
wife could never have dissembled successfully. So
he was not worried.

As he sat he brooded over the facts of the case
once more.

He began by mulling over the personnel list
again, thinking of the meager facts he had gleaned,
and the impressions swirling in his mind.

He suddenly remembered that the American
flag had been flying when he arrived that morning,
and made a note to ask what their practices were to
raise and lower the flag. Would they have left it up
all weekend?

At some point, Dantan realized that Judy's murmurings had ceased and that there were two voices now in the salon. A moment later, Judy knocked on his door. "Miri Winter is here," she announced. "I've invited her to stay for supper. I had wanted her to come over earlier, when she first called, but she said she wanted to go home and paint for a couple of hours, the only chance she has on weekdays. Do you mind? I know you're usually bored with my American friends, but since she works right there where 'it' happened, I thought you might be willing."

Dantan considered for a moment the ethics of this, socializing with a potential suspect in his new case, but since the probability that the killer was Miri Winter was statistically zero, and she might have something interesting to offer, he told his wife he was pleased, and joined the ladies.

On the whole Dantan was quite happy with the changes to his life which he had effected since January of that year, nineteen-hundred-fifty-four. Judy was amusing as well as sexy. She was learning to cook the French way by taking a course at the *Cordon Bleu* and watching their elderly *bonne* Germaine. Judy got on very well with Germaine, who not only cooked well but kept their apartment immaculate and smelling fragrantly of beeswax and fresh flowers. To have come to work for them after the oppressive autocratic treatment she had received from her former mistress *Madame* Fleuris was, for poor old Germaine, a new lease on life. And Judy had a good rapport with his comrades from the Sixth Section and the P.J., chattered with their wives, presided gracefully when he invited a higher-up and wife to dine with them. Her French was getting better all the time, but he despaired of her ever losing the unmistakable American accent.

Her excessive and girlish American wardrobe was somewhat of an embarassment to him, but she was learning what was chic and had acquired a few garments in which she could appear anywhere, though she needed practice in carrying them with panache.

His father-in-law had bought the couple a car. Mr Kugel couldn't conceive of anyone getting around without one. Futile for Dantan to try to persuade him that most Parisians didn't own a car, and managed to get from one end of the city to another by Metro, by bus, by taxi, by bicycle or by Velo-Solex. But once they had the car, a black Renault, he and Judy enjoyed it, taking a few weekend trips to the country, where they stayed at a small inn, and ate delicious country food.

In sum, Dantan had not begun to be bored, as Pilieu and others had teased he would.

Dantan, Judy and Miri sat at one end of the long mahogany dining table, Dantan at the head, the women on either side. Germaine was serving, grinning one of her rare broad smiles at having another of her favorite former boarders at table.

The table had a small history: Judy and her mother were determined to find an authentic antique dining set, not only a large table but carved chairs, sideboard and a china-chest on legs, and had gone from flea markets to antiques shops and had studied classifieds, without finding something they thought was suitable.

Judy had wanted to buy the whole suite at her old *pension*, but *Monsieur* Fleuris was not open to offers; any offers. He and his mistress didn't need the money, thank *le bon Dieu*! Her next idea was to purchase much of the furniture, not just the dining pieces, from the apartment which had been seized during the war from the Maisel family after they were deported, but the putative owner was still renting out the place furnished – almost fifteen years after the war – and would part with nothing.

Meanwhile the young couple had been using a folding bridge table and folding chairs the Kugels had shipped from America, along with the other household goods which Judy's mother felt her daughter could not survive marriage without.

Then Jean-Jacques Pilieu solved their problem. After an invitation to dine there, when the subject of dining-room furniture came up as they were eating at a folding-table, Pilieu presented his solution to Dantan. Pilieu suggested that they look at his mother's dining furniture. It had come down from his grandmother, and possibly his great-grandmother, and had been kept in good repair and immaculately polished through the generations. Since his father had died, his mother had ceased preparing meals for anyone except him and his brother and she preferred that they eat in the kitchen at the wooden work-table where she had rolled out pastries in happier days.

His mother could use the money, and she didn't need such a big table. He was sure she would be happy to make a deal. Dantan had some qualms about taking something that would always remind him of his unearned, perhaps undeserved, wealth contrasted with his friend's situation, but when he told Judy about the offer she was ecstatic and was in love with the furniture even before seeing it. For her part, *Madame* Pilieu was glad to get rid of the old suite, she was tired of being reminded of episodes of younger happier days every time she sat down to table. And the money was very welcome.

Now he and Judy would start creating experiences that might become a burden to recall in later years, a painful thought he immediately suppressed.

Dantan was not displeased that Miri Winter had joined them for dinner. She might come up with a useful piece of information or two.

Before Dantan could say hello, Miri blurted out, "Colonel Ritchie is terrifically furious at me for calling in the French police when I found the body. He wanted to hush it up and only have the Army investigate it. He said Kitty was correct in wanting to wait for him to arrive, so that they could keep the incident within the Army, bring in Army investigators and keep the Frenchies out. Charlie told me this, because he thought the colonel was going to ask him to fire me, but before he could do so, Charlie told him how useful I was around the office, and the colonel relented. Which by the way is a joke as I have almost nothing to do. I type a few endorsements a day, and file a few things. But Charlie likes me, for some reason," She laughed. "Maybe it's because I'm such a good customer for his home-made brownies!"

Dantan could understand the colonel's feelings; but from what he had gleaned so far from Chief Inspector Goulette, the chief inspector and the U.S. Army brass on the case had already spoken on the telephone and were working out a *modus operandi* between them. As long as the Army appeared to be in charge, they didn't care who actually did the work.

Once they showed up in Paris they would be happy
to take any forensic analyses, and notes on interviews, which the French could provide. And while
they were going to do their own questioning, they
were not trying to tie the hands of the *Police Judiciare*.

"The murder occurred on French territory, not
American," he said to the girls. "Only the American
Embassy is considered American territory."

"Well he is in a big hurry for the brass to arrive
from the U.S. Army Criminal Investigation Command so he can kick you guys out."

"We'll do what we can to help," Dantan said
calmly.

"Do you think the black market dealing in liquor has anything to do with it?" asked Miri.

Dantan shrugged. "It seems to be well-known
throughout the office, so if Lieutenant Morgan was
doing something about it, he was not handling a clan-
destine operation. Unless, of course, the black
marketeering extends beyond what we have
learned."

"What is this about a black market?" Judy asked
eagerly.

"Oh, just that a woman supervisor and some
oafs from the machine-room go to the PX every day,
buy a quart of Scotch, which they are allowed to do,
and cartons of cigarettes, and then resell it to French
bars. Carolene, the supervisor, tried to get me to

buy my allowance and let her resell it, but I refused."

"And she would take the profit?" Judy said indignantly.

"That's not the point. I wouldn't do it because it's not right. She would have paid me something, but I said no. There's one soldier who buys his liquor allowance and gives it to Carolene so she'll lend him her car when he's racked up enough credits with her. He's infatuated with Jackie Harris, the civilian files-manager, who dashes off to Germany every other minute to buy more antique furniture for her collection, and he's trying to make out with her, but so far has had no luck."

"He must really be in love if he keeps driving all the way to Germany and back! Ugh!"

Dantan mused, "I'll bet Kitty Hill knows more about the staff than she's telling. Has she ever gossiped to you?"

"She did for awhile, not that I paid much attention. Now of course, I wish I had. She's always running in and telling Charlie stuff. Charlie loves gossip too, he's like a little old lady. And I know Kitty's always poking around in the colonel's personnel files, I've seen her doing it when I came in especially early. Maybe we could have become friends, but then something happened..."

"What happened?"

Miri was uncomfortable going on and had to

be coaxed to continue. Dantan thought there was always the chance of learning something relevant, and Judy loved gossip, relevant or not.

On the Monday in May after Miri had been ordered out of Reid Hall and had agreed to move in with Renee, she told Charlie she would be moving into a big old apartment near the *Place des Vosges*. She did not mention that she was being dispossessed by Reid Hall.

There was little new gossip that morning so Miri's impending move made it into the news circulating around the office, especially since Monday was Charlie's brownie day and just about everyone dropped in to his office at least once.

That afternoon even Jackie Harris dropped in. She had heard Miri was moving and offered to help. "I have a big truck and would be glad to give you a hand."

This was a bolt out of the blue! And what a really nice gesture since they had hardly ever spoken with each other since Miri began work at FOUSAP.

Jackie and Miri arranged the move for Wednesday after work. Miri had a lot to move. Besides a few clothes, some books, art materials, an easel, and the Maisel photographs, she had the numerous paintings she had done since she had obtained the photographs. She also had some stretched blank canvases. So she was grateful for the opportunity of moving the canvases without spending a lot of money (nothing, in fact) and without worrying that they would be damaged.

Jackie, as good as her word, showed up at Reid Hall on Wednesday evening with her truck, and helped Miri lug the canvases down the stairs and outside. Seymour had left Paris for Garmisch again, so he couldn't help. Renee had not offered to help as she was too busy with her research.

Jackie was in an exuberant mood as they bounced along the streets of Paris. She loved her truck and she loved driving it around Paris. She also loved talking about her antiques.

She informed Miri that her specialty was Biedermeier. Miri had never heard of this style, so Jackie happily proceeded to tell her more than she wanted to know about its origins, the difference between the German and Austrian versions, and the fact that this was not a particularly popular style just yet, so some exquisite pieces were available at throwaway prices, particularly in Germany, where the owners still desperately needed money for food.

"Is this all horribly dull for you?" Jackie laughed.

"Oh no, it's very interesting."

"You're very sweet. Pretty too."

Miri did not react much; people were always telling her that, but usually adding things like, "You could be a beautiful girl if you would just dress better" (Judy's mother), "Get your hair cut" (Renee), "Stop talking about Existentialism" (various boys she met at the American Club) and so on.

After they had lugged everything up the stairs into the large but decrepit apartment – Renee was not around, but had given Miri a key – Jackie invited Miri to drop in to her place sometime and see her Biedermeier collection. Miri thanked her politely but with no intention of doing so.

When Renee returned to the apartment later, Miri told her of Jackie's help and her invitation to see a collection of Biedermeier antiques. Renee proceeded to lecture her on the importance of an artist of becoming familiar with other manifestations of the culture of a given period as well as painting, to understand the philosophy and emotional underpinnings of an age. Being shown a collection of Biedermeier by an ardent collector would be an invaluable introduction to life in Germany and Austria in the first half of the nineteenth century. She should also look into the school of Robert Morris in England....

Miri and Jackie had carried all Miri's things into the large back room Renee had allotted to her. It was somewhat dark for painting, but Miri had hopes that Renee wouldn't mind if she set up an easel in the big dining room. That room contained only a small table and two chairs, and promised to have good north light.

Even though the place was dreary and the bath-tub was in the kitchen, one of those small ones like Seymour's with a seat in it and a hand-shower, she was surprisingly excited at the change of residence. She could walk to the *Place des Vosges* every day! And there were interesting old buildings to sketch. And she might even draw some of the bearded bent old men in black in the neighborhood, although they still depressed her.

A few days after the move, a Saturday, Miri trekked over to Jackie's cavernous apartment near *Châtelet,* and not seeing a doorbell, rapped hard on the door.

After a short delay, Jackie opened the door a crack, blinking and peering out with squinting eyes. The apartment was dark, as if all the shutters were closed, and the drapes drawn. "Oh it's you, Miri," Jackie murmured.

Just then, Kitty Hill appeared at the door be-hind Jackie, looking disheveled, her hair a mess and her blouse buttoned incorrectly. "What are you do-ing here?" she demanded in an uncharacteristically unfriendly way.

Miri stammered, "Jackie invited me to drop in sometime to see the Biedermeiers."

Jackie gave a laugh, and opened the door wider. "Come in, come in!"

Miri caught a glimpse of a sleeping alcove; the

bed-covers were all mussed. And over a kitchen chair near the bed was a pair of lace-frilled pink panties.

To Kitty, Jackie said imperiously, "Make us some coffee, Kitten."

"Oh don't bother." Miri felt very embarassed. "I can't stay long."

"Well you can stay long enough for coffee and have a whirlwind tour of the chests and chairs and cabinets and one very special *prie-dieu*." She led Miri to a round table with concavely curved legs and gold medallions above each leg. "Walnut and birch," Jackie said like a museum-guide, "early nineteenth century, Viennese." She gave a deep laugh from her throat. "I paid very little for this – it required restoration, which I did myself – but I expect to sell it in ten or fifteen years for thousands of dollars."

Kitty silently set the table with a pad, then a round lacy cloth. She retrieved a steaming porcelain pot of coffee, three delicate china cups and saucers, and a little plate of miniature *palmiers*. She had rebuttoned her blouse and combed her hair. Miri presumed she had put her panties back on.

After that day, Kitty didn't run into Miri's office very often with tidbits of gossip.

Judy giggled. "Come up and see my Biedermeiers sometime. She probably was thinking of dumping 'Kitten'."

Miri said glumly, "I feel sick that she moved all my stuff. She carried most of the canvases down the Reid Hall stairs out to the truck, and unloaded them and carried them up the stairs to Renee's place, and she handled everything very carefully."

"That was very nice of her," Judy suddenly spoke up. "What's so terrible about that?"

"Oh nothing, I guess. I just don't feel like returning any favors to her. And I can't look at Kitty anymore without remembering seeing her at Jackie's, all mussed up and her panties hanging over the chair."

"So your boss Charlie Nugent, whom you describe as a fount of gossip, never mentioned the girls' special friendship?"

"Not to me. I don't think he even knew about it, or I would surely have overheard him telling someone. All he chuckled over was Private Dennis Bernardi's infatuation with her, and how he follows her all over. So Dennis obviously doesn't know it's a hopeless cause. He's the butt of a lot of jokes because his infatuation is so one-sided. And Charlie's roommate, Peter Parnes, who keeps giving Charlie and everyone else updates on Dennis Bernardi's latest hopeless efforts didn't seem to know. Charlie doesn't exactly pry, but he hears a lot of gossip when everyone drops in for his brownies."

"How did Charlie Nugent get along with Lieutenant Morgan? Any conflicts or disagreements that you know of between them?" Dantan asked, obviously following his own line of thought.

"Not at all. Charlie gets along with everybody. He's everyone's grandma."

"Did Lieutenant Morgan ever drop in for brownies?"

"No, but Kitty did all the time, and would take an extra one for each of the officers."

"Those brownies make my mouth water," Judy giggled. "I'm going to bake some tomorrow, and show Germaine how to do it. Miri you'll have to come back for some after work."

Miri said, "I've got to get some painting done. And I eat too many of them when Charlie brings them in. Thanks anyway."

"So Charlie Nugent is Gossip Central," Dantan chuckled. "I'll have to talk to him some more. But you probably hear a great deal when the door is left open between your two offices, to say nothing of what he must have told you directly?"

"Oh yes, if Charlie doesnt know something, nobody does."

"I can't believe no one knew about Kitty Hill and Jackie Harris," Judy said, getting right into the gossiping spirit despite her lack of acquaintance with most of the players. "Especially that Dennis Bernardi. He must be unusually obtuse. He didn't seem that dumb the time he was at my dinner party. Maybe you should tell Dennis about his beloved's proclivities. Save him wasting his time and even save him some grief."

Miri remembered with embarassment her own earlier infatuation with Jamie Guardini. She would have been spared the humiliation if someone had told her about his "proclivities" before she tried to climb into his bed. But he had been very sweet about it, and they had remained friends.

"But suppose she's AC/DC and will come around eventually? I don't know about him, only what Charlie has said, joking how infatuated he is with Jackie. And he didn't seem to realize it was an ironic joke."

Dantan was still following his own line of thought. He asked Miri, "The American flag outside FOUSAP. It was raised in the morning and lowered in the evening?"

"Yes, unless it was raining hard, then they didn't put it up."

"Who raised it in the morning?"

"Lieutenant Morgan. I don't think he ever missed a day since I started there, but the instructions were that if he couldn't make it to the office then the next highest officer, in our case, Sergeant Carr Southwood, would do it."

"And did the lieutenant lower it in the evening?"

"Whichever military man was the last one out."

"Miri, think back now to this morning when you got there and Kitty Hill was barring the door. Had the flag been raised?"

"Yes. I remember that distinctly, because there was no breeze at all and I noticed how it was hanging limply, not flapping like a flag should."

"When you left on Friday evening before was the flag still flying?"

"I'm not sure. Because I left on the minute of five-thirty, one of the first ones out the door."

Dantan took her down the list of staff, civilian and military, but she had little to offer about any of them, other than the rumor she had heard from Charlie that Vic Logan's wife had not really had a medical emergency at home, but had wanted to leave Vic without making a scandal for him at the office.

"And the Army gave her emergency leave just like that?"

"I guess so. I wasn't there yet, But Vic Logan is too valuable to them to start making a fuss over whether his wife was really entitled to emergency medical leave or not. So what if she wasn't? What would they have gained by questioning it, and losing him?"

Germaine had cleared the table while they were talking and now brought out a big bowl of fruit compote, a platter of cheeses with small pieces of *ba-guette*, as well as a plateful of American-style choco-late-chip cookies, which Judy had taught her how to make. She still had a supply of the American choco-late chips Miri had been clever enough to bring her from the PX on a previous visit, but made sure to hint that their supply was running low and that there-fore Miri would have to come back sooner than she did after the previous visit and bring some bags of chocolate chips. "Please don't wait for another mur-der!" she giggled.

Miri squirmed at the joke.

During their lighthearted banter, Dantan thought of some questions to ask at FOUSAP the next day, and excused himself to go to his study and write them down. He took two chocolate-chip cook-ies with him to go with the *filtre* Germaine would soon be bringing him After having his coffee, he would go to the FOUSAP building to prowl around.

11

The taxi dropped Dantan on the street. He didn't want to be driven ino the courtyard although there were no cars parked there now. He crossed the cobblestones, mounted the wide stone steps, and let himself in the front door. The American flag was not on its flagpole.

The pale marble of the ground floor had been thoroughly scrubbed, but looking at it closely, Dantan could discern a faint pinkish color, possibly the dry remains of blood, in some veins of the marble. A workman expert with marble would no doubt be called in to clean it more thoroughly. The cloakroom had been straightened up as it had been before Colonel Ritchie required it as a temporary office. Folding chairs had been folded up and stacked against a wall. Dantan gave it a quick glance, wondering if the killer had concealed himself there until all the other personnel had left, except the lieutenant. Nobody would have been retrieving coats or umbrellas that day.

He went down the back stairs to the machine-room, but could not get in. Vic Logan had evidently locked it before leaving. In any case Dantan wanted to speak with Logan again the next day, and would take another look around at that time.

Dantan proceeded up the wide spiraling staircase to the first floor. The officers' offices and Kitty Hill's on his right, were locked. To the left of the staircase were the offices of Craig Jayes, Charles Nugent, and Miri Winter. All these doors were open, including the passage between the Nugent office and the secretary's. If that passage were left open anyone in one office could easily hear anything being said in the other.

Not a single piece of paper was to be seen. Each desk was clean. The secretary's typewriter had a black cover over it.

Abnormally neat. That's how it struck him. No work in evidence, no human untidiness.

He mounted the wide spiral staircase slowly. The medical examiner suggested the possibilty, though slim, that the lieutenant might not have died as soon as he was struck, and perhaps somehow had moved himself enough to roll over the edge of the stairs and down to the ground floor, where he had been found sprawled at the foot of the stairs.

He looked in on Jackie Harris' cell-like office; shipshape. Similarly, the larger office next door shared by Private Bernardi, Private Parnes, and Sergeant Southwood. All three desks were clear; no signs of mess, or even work, were visible.

Up one flight more, and Dantan first examined the conference room. The overhead light, a crystal chandelier, was on. The cleaning woman was at work. She was fat and aging, wore a faded gray housedress and coverall apron and was flapping around in the carpet-slippers that were ubiquitous among laboring women in Paris. Her gray hair was tucked up in a bun with wisps hanging down, years of hard work etched into her face. She looked up when Dantan entered, greeted him politely, "*Bon soir, M'sieur*", then continued with her work. "*Bon soir, Madame.* I am Inspector Alphone Dantan of the *Police Judiciare.*" He proferred his identification. She barely glanced at it. It was possible she could not read.

She was wielding a long-handled feather duster and was carefully extending it behind each of the file cabinets, which stood about a meter away from the mirrored wall, the space presumably left to protect the mirrors. Noticing that Dantan just stood there observing her, she sighed, "Just imagine, when I was a young girl I was so slim I could have slipped right behind these cabinets to do my cleaning!"

Dantan was very struck by this observation. The space between the mirrored wall and the backs of the file-cabinets was about a meter, and had been left, presumably, to avoid inadvertent damage to the mirrored walls. Now he saw that a person sufficiently small and slim could have been hiding behind the file cabinets -- perhaps with the murderer! Bearing a fatal implement, such as a hammer or a wrench, at a convenient moment, he could have quietly slipped out from his hiding-place and bashed the lieutenant on the head. The trouble with that theory was that the conference room was on the *second* floor, and the body was found on the ground floor.

"May I ask you a few questions, Madame?"

"*Bien sûr, Monsieur.*" But she kept on with her dusting.

"When did you work here last?"

"Last Monday. I come in one night a week."

"And how do you get into the building? Do you have your own key?"

"No, the boss drives us to our jobs, drops us off, and opens each door. When he picks us up he locks the doors behind him."

"And is it the same night of the week each week?"

"Yes. If one of the ladies can't make it then

someone fills in for her that night."

"So the last time you worked in this building was one week ago?"

"That's right."

Dantan walked slowly around the conference room, but noticed nothing out of the ordinary. It too had been cleaned, the table, the floor... "Did you clean any unusual debris or dirt in this room this evening, *Madame?*"

"No, *M'sieur,* nothing special. It was cleaner than usual, if anything."

He would have to find out who did clean it up and see if they remembered anything "special."

The next morning, Tuesday, Dantan returned to the FOUSAP mansion. He wanted to talk with Jackie Harris again. The more he thought over the tale that she was driving all the way to Germany and back to buy out-of-favor old furniture, the less he believed it. An inspector would have to ask her to produce receipts for these supposed purchases, as well as examine her passport for stamps showing when and where she had entered and departed a country.

When he entered Jackie Harris' office, she was sitting primly at her desk, turning the pages of a bound computer listing. Small, thin and dark, with sharp features. A pointed nose, a pointed chin, even her ears were slightly pointed. And she had a sharp manner about her too. If this were the cinema she would be a perfect suspect!

"You sometimes drive to Munich and back? More than nine-hundred kilometers each way?"

"I do. I don't need much sleep, Inspector. And I love to drive. Especially on the Autobahn. I go faster than they allow, technically, but nobody interferes."

"So you go to Munich pretty often?"

"Not often enough to suit me! The finds there are unbelievable. Biedermeier furniture is out of fashion, though I'm counting on it coming back in with my help, and a lot of people in Germany and Austria need the money just to live."

"Can you think of any reason anyone here would have had for killing the lieutenant?"

"None. He wasn't a likable man, but on the other hand, he was fair and even-handed. And I never saw him in a single dispute with anyone. He was known to be curt with anyone who arrived late to the office. Hardly a motive for murder."

"What time did you leave the office Friday evening?"

"Right on time. Five-thirty."

"And then you left for Munich?"

"Not right away. I wanted to work on my truck first."

"You were having a problem with it?"

"No, Inspector, but there is always something that can be tinkered with and improved. And I like doing so."

This woman was definitely an oddity. Mad about the internal combusion engine, he had heard. Could take apart any engine, tune it up, do whatever it needed, detect the source of strange sounds.... If anyone possessed an array of tools with which to bash the lieutenant on the head, it would be she!

Dantan sighed. He would have liked to be skilled with auto engines. He had never had the opportunity before. Could never afford a vehicle. He had been hoping to save on his inspector's salary to buy a little *quatre chevaux*. With his marriage, his income was greatly augmented with a generous allowance from Judy's father, and the gift of a car.

Upon leaving Jackie Harris' office he was waylaid by Kitty to tell him that the colonel wished to meet with him.

The colonel seemed to have shrunk since Dantan spoke with him the previous morning. He was still in full dress uniform but had lost his panache and swagger. His face sagged and he looked very sad.

"Inspector, I asked to speak with you rather than your chief because I was getting impatient with all that translating going on for every little remark."

Dantan nodded.

"Tell me straight. Who are your suspects at this point?"

"Theoretically, anyone working in this building might have done it. We've ruled out anyone from the outside as highly unlikely; you can see why. But as to individuals who had access and motive, I can't say yet." And he wouldn't, not until he felt it was time to make an arrest.

"As I told your chief," the colonel said, "I have called in U.S. Army investigative officers. Until they arrive, and immerse themselves in this case, I would like to hear whatever you French find or learn. You will be expected to turn the evidence over to them in any event."

"Understood. I, for one, am not concealing anything. We just don't know much at this time." As Dantan said these words he thought he detected a slight flicker of emotion pass over the colonel's face. He found that intriguing. He wondered if the colonel himself knew something he wasn't telling the French investigators. "Do you yourself have any ideas? Motives, for instance?"

Again a flicker of emotion. Dantan was now sure that the colonel knew or suspected something. But he didn't press the point. That was for his chief to do. Probably the colonel wanted to keep something in reserve to give the American Army investigators an edge when they began.

"What about one of the French nationals?" the colonel tossed off. "You must know they all hate us."

"Every girl who works in the machine room has been questioned," Dantan said noncommittally, although it angered him that a whole group was treated as if every member thought alike. "None of them had occasion to go upstairs and none of them was seen doing so."

"You're not ruling them out, though, are you?" The colonel sounded as if he would make sure the American investigators did not rule them out!

"We're not ruling anyone out unless there's certainty to do so." Not even you, Colonel Ritchie, Dantan smiled to himself. Although the colonel was low on his list of suspects. If there were anything unpleasant to be done, the colonel was the type to get someone else to do it.

The colonel shrugged. The protocols he had sternly laid down had already been broken – in one day.

Vic Logan was rushing from one machine to another when Dantan arrived downstairs. He gave Dantan an angry look, as if to say, "Can't you see I'm too busy doing the work of the United States Government to bother with you?" But since Dantan approached and stood his ground patiently, Logan eventually, with a bad grace, said, "Well?"

"The night of the murder you were, you said, the last person to leave the building."

"Nothing unusual about that. Happens almost all the time."

"But then you came back later."

Logan gave him a blank look.

"Did you leave and then come back?"

"Sometimes I go for a bite to eat, then come back, if I'm going to be working especially late."

"Well did you do that the evening of Sixteenth of July? Lastft Friday night."

"I may have. I don't recall one way or the other."

"When you do go for something to eat, with the intention of returning, where do you go for your meal?"

"Snack, inspector, not a meal. There's a bistro in the neighborhood."

"Snack, then," Dantan smiled. "*Casse-croute.* If you did go away for awhile, and then come back, is it certain that you would have gone to the bistro?"

"It is not certain," Logan snapped, "And I would appreciate your not wasting any more of my time."

Dantan took the name and location of the bistro. He had no reason to disbelieve the next-door chauffeur that Logan had driven off and then come back.

Dantan decided to have a proper *déjeuner* at home. He had left his copies of the case-reports at home and now went back to look them over again Judy was there, to his surprise, as she usually flitted around town during the day, knowing he rarely came home in the middle of the day. Germaine assured them she could put together a real *déjeuner* since he was there to enjoy it and he and his wife sat down, somewhat later, to a savory *pot au feu.*

"I'm quitting the *Cordon Bleu.*"

Dantan took this news calmly. Germaine was doing most of the cooking anyway, even American dishes such as chocolate-chip cookies, which Judy had taught her how to make and which he found quite appealing.

Husband and wife took a satisfying love interlude and nap together after the mid-day meal, and Dantan only departed for his office once the workmen returned and resumed their banging and drilling.

The chief inspector was now juggling Colonel Ritchie's demands and those of crimes elsewhere in Paris which required his attention. Dantan spoke briefly with Pilieu. He asked him to speak with the concierge at Jackie Harris' building, Pilieu had already done so. *Mademoiselle* Harris was a slightly notorious character, with all her comings and goings in her big red truck. But she tipped well, and was well-liked.

"It's the truck I'm interested in," Dantan said. "See if anyone saw *Mademoiselle* Harris working on her truck on the evening of the Sixteenth of July. She would undoubtedly do that sort of thing in the courtyard where she habitually parked it. If anyone saw her working on the truck, try to get an estimate of the time and how long she took."

Pilieu came back with an interesting report. He had found in *Mademoiselle* Harris' building that invaluable type of eyewitness, a housebound old lady.

"The Mademoiselle with the big truck rattled in," she had told Pilieu, much excited to be interviewed by such an interested young man. "She jumped out of her truck, ran upstairs, came back again with a golf-bag, and some time after, a large brown car pulled into the courtyard with a skid, the *Mademoiselle* flung her golf-bag into the trunk, then jumped into the car next to the driver and they sped off."

"And the truck remained there?"

"I don't know. My niece had come over soon after. bringing a really nice dinner, and by the time we had eaten, and my niece had left, and I looked out the window again, the truck was gone. But I don't know when."

Pilieu was delighted to have come across an

unusual fact. He did not believe he had the level of ability Dantan had.

Pilieu joshed his friend for "taking over the department," but was not displeased that that was the case. He liked Dantan very much, and he himself was a more plodding type, not likely to take charge of much. After his long lethargy and depression, Dantan had snapped out of it with his new assignment to the P.J. last year. And Pilieu took satisfaction in the fact that he had been instrumental in getting Dantan his original job as interpreter at the P.J.

12

Privates Seymour Levin and Nate Roth, their long legs sprawled from necesssity beside the formica table on which they had set up a chessboard, were concentrating intently on the game. This despite the din and smoke in the Garmisch base canteen, and the comments from the occasional kibitzers who dropped by to oversee the game and offer advice, even if they didn't know how to play chess. It was Monday evening, July 19th.

Private Levin had a dark gaze which seemed to take in more than it let out. He was in Garmisch investigating, in a low-keyed, inconspicuous way, some irregularities in the FOUSAP reports coming out of the machine-rooms in Garmisch and Paris. A superior officer in Paris, Lieutenant John Morgan, had been made aware of Levin's suspicions and had asked Seymour to nose around. A private who lugged printouts, emptied the chip-box when a key-punch machine ceased to function, someone who did whatever lowly task wherever he was needed, was far less conspicuous than brinnging in big guns from headquarters for a full-fledged investigation. Colonel Ritchie, for one, was looking forward to retirement soon, and would not have wanted his management of things scrutinized too carefully. Lieutenant Morgan understood this, and had felt he could handle the situation and bring it to a discreet but successful conclusion.

Seymour and Nate were deep into their chess game when a soldier they knew slightly rushed over and excitedly announced that a lieutenant in the Paris finance office had been found murdered! Right in the office! No suspect yet.

The news was already all over the base as Lieutenant Morgan, who was well-known, at least by reputation, had been stationed at Garmisch before his transfer to Paris a few months previous.

Seymour Levin and Nate Roth, slight acquaintances at Harvard, had become good friends after discovering themselves on the same army base in Garmisch. Most of the enlisted men were not exactly educated, in fact, many were ignorant bigots. Most of the college men, especially Ivy Leaguers, were officers. They might be ignorant bigots, too, but their bigotry was displayed with panache and a veneer of sophistication.

Nate had had to drop out of college for a year because his father was dying. When he returned to school it was to a city institution, to save money and be nearer to his mother.

Seymour and Nate had both declined officer training in favor of a shorter period of service, remained lowly privates. They both hated the Army: rednecks seemed everywhere; supercilious officers were basically stupid; food so bad that they had each lost more than twenty pounds, Nate from an already lean and lanky frame, Seymour from a large build which hardly reflected the loss of weight. They wanted to spend as little time in the service of their country as they could legally manage. Thankfully, the Korean War had ended before they were drafted; they were spared having to fight, although some men were still being shipped there.

The two became part of a regular base poker game. Seymour almost always won big pots. He was not only smarter than the other players, but had mastered a frozen poker-face which gave away nothing. Nate was smart, too, but found it more difficult to conceal his emotions. In order to maintain a degree of civility with the other G.I.'s, Seymour refrained from playing in every game. He didn't want to take all their money. Sometimes he placed chess, another game where he usually beat all takers, although Nate was a worthy opponent. The few chess players among the enlisted men kept coming back for more, hoping to vanquish him. One of them was so desperate to win that he tried to get Seymour drunk during a game, hoping this would disrupt his judgment. The game resulted in a draw.

Then, during the previous December, they became absorbed with a problem Nate suspected in Ordnance. He himself had a narrowly-defined clerical job, but people with more opportunity to observe, had told him of their suspicions. Put simply, heavy expensive equipment, valuable on the black market, was disappearing in quantity and frequently. This in itself was not news; theft was a perennial problem. What made the present occasion different was that the inventories failed to reflect the items that had disappeared. That is, they were listed on bills of lading when the shipments first came in, but some time between their arrival and their disappearance they were no longer listed anywhere. It was as if the shipping documents had been written in invisible ink.

Nate surmised that records were being tampered with to cover up the disappearances. He tried to drop hints to superiors to start an investigation. But nobody wanted to make waves, especially with a low likelihood of success. Officers did not want anything to ruffle the calm surface of their days or their reputations.

Whatever the Army was losing, America could afford it. America had won the war, it was supporting most of Europe – not only its allies, but its former enemies, and those supposed allies who had given up without a fight – yet it could still afford to treat its military better than any in the world. The value of the missing materiels was a just a drop in the ocean. There were leaks of materiel everywhere. And yesterday's heroes might be among today's black marketeers. Why bother?

The trouble was that Seymour and Nate had Jewish consciences. They would have felt guilty if they had looked the other way, although that was the most prudent thing to do. Next best was to try to solve what was going on without bringing in the big guns who would kick up a fuss and humiliate the local officers.

Up to this point, each had done what he could without stirring up a hornet's nest. Nate took frequent nightly strolls with one of his blondes, walking as close to the fenced-in storage facilities as he could get. He was on the lookout for movement of vehicles that might represent goods going out. But the only signs of life he ever spotted were the guards, slouching and smoking and giving the couple a friendly wave.

Seymour, a clerk assigned to the Garmisch data processing division, where endless decks of punched cards were fed into printers to spew forth endless oversized pages of reports, tried to pick up clues to falsified records. Someone was supposed to examine these reports, but most of the time they were just ripped from their carbons and put into binders by lowly privates like himself, and then shelved on top of the previous set of reports. Copies of everything, of course, together with their associated decks of cards, were packaged weekly and sent to the Paris finance office to be consolidated, along with similar reports from other European bases. Paris did further consolidations, and presumably, some analysis, and forwarded the results to yet another consolidating finance office, this one in Peachtree, Georgia, where further far-flung reports came in and further consolidations performed. These reports were then sent on to Washington, where it was extremely unlikely that anyone ever looked at them again, and if they had, would not have understood one line.

Seymour suspected that the reports were being tampered with, but so far he had not figured out how.

"Maybe we're tilting at windmills," Nate had said quietly early in their quest. "Or holding a thumb in a dike which has sprouted leaks all over."

"Both probably true," Seymour chuckled. "But how can we give up? There are only three alternatives: one, give up; two, go on as we are, doing what we personally can, without shaking up the brass, that is, without getting into trouble; or, three, reporting this up in a way that will bring in the big guns."

"And a curse upon our heads," said Nate. "It won't do anyone any good if we got into trouble. Let's keep going as we are for awhile at least, and then review where we've gotten."

Seymour had assented, for then. Now, he fervently wished he had taken a more aggressive road.

So Seymour would continue to do, was to give microscopic attention to all aspects of the activities in the machine-room in Garmisch, looking for anomalies. He scrutinized forms, often filled in by hand, which were the keypunch-operators' raw material. He looked at verifications, scanned reports selected at random – it would have been impossible to look at them all – hardly knowing what he was looking for, hoping impressions swirling in his deep memory would click on some insight.

The supervisor of the machine room, a sergeant, was not grateful for this voluntary oversight. In fact, he frequently grumbled that Private Levin was just "getting in the way."

The sergeant's annoyance with Private Levin led to an event immensely pleasing to the latter: in late

January he was suddenly transferred to Paris! The scuttlebutt that was that the sergeant was intent on getting rid of Private Levin without any hint that was trying to boot him out, which would have raised questions he preferred not be raised, and the way he had avoided that was to aid in having the private sent to a very desirable location, rather than exile, and what could be more desirable than Paris! This announced to the curious that Private Levin was being rewarded, not punished.

Now he would be able to get as close to Miri Winter as she would let him. Although she tended to be skittish when hugged or fondled Seymour was hoping she would get used to it once he was around more often and would get to like it.

Nate would keep strolling past the storage facilities.

They would, of course, stay in touch.

Once Seymour was installed in Paris, he tried to talk with the lieutenant then there, Lieutenant Spear, about what he suspected. The lieutenant stonewalled him. The lieutenant pointed out that the chain of command was through Sergeant Carr Southwood. Seymour disliked the sergeant, but more than that, he mistrusted him. Arrogantly stupid, thought Seymour, a supercilious bastard would not listen with the intent of doing anything about a problem. He might very well make a problem worse, or at the very least, do his best to cover it up.

So Seymour decided to bypass not only the sergeant, but the lieutenant, and approach the colonel directly.

The colonel wouldn't talk to him.

Through the colonel's secretary, Kitty Hill, Seymour was advised to take up any issues he had with his next in command. There was an implication of insubordination when Seymour persisted in trying to talk with the colonel, until he was told flatly to get lost.

But Seymour thought it might not be a coincidence that within a few weeks Leutenant Spear was transferrred out, and a new lieutenant, named Morgan, was transferred in, from Garmisch. Before Seymour was able to approach Morgan, the lieutenant had made it widely known in FOUSAP that he was an ardent chess-player and that he had heard about Private Seymour Levin at Garmisch, that he was one of the top players there, and the lieutenant would like to have a game with him.

The two began playing regularly after work at a cafe, and thus had a perfectly discreet way to discuss sensitive topics without other staff suspecting it.

The colonel was unhappy that an officer and an enlisted man were fraternizing, but in all other respects Lieutenant Morgan was perfectly correct.

So on this point the colonel looked the other way.

By July, Seymour and Nate had just about given up on discovering evidence working from their own vantage-points. Seymour did feel he had a listening ear in Lieutenant Morgan, that was all (quite a bit, actually) that he, as a private, could hope for.

Seymour felt sick at the thought of the lieutenant's murder, and the possibility that it was related to what he had been delving into. Perhaps Morgan had gotten an idea of who was involved, and confronted the person on whom his suspicions focused. Seymour had felt fortunate that he could confide in the lieutenant at their informal get-togethers over chess. He didn't trust Sergeant Southwood, his next-in-command.

Seymour had laid out the facts that he knew to the lieutenant, together with his theory, and the lieutenant, Seymour surmised, may have been doing some tough questioning, getting close to the perpetrators of the fraud they had uncovered, stirring up fears which led to his murder.

Nate was equally dismayed at the news.

"I've got to get to Paris as soon as possible," Seymour told Nate. "I think the sergeant will agree that I can leave in time to get a train to Munich connecting with one to Paris which would get me in tomorrow night. He knows I'm working on something he doesn't want to know about. That leg of the trip is over eight hours. Any chance you can get leave to join me?"

"Not a chance."

Seymour was worried about Miri too. She was not clever at protecting her flank. Suppose she knew something she didn't know she knew, and the wrong person found out? Someone had gone to the extreme and already killed... And even if Miri knew nothing, being in the vicinity of a killer was not healthy for a young girl.

After checking timetables, Seymour saw that the the earliest train from Garmisch to Munich did not arrive in time to make the connection to Paris. He would have to take a later train.

Before he made his late morning train out of Garmisch, he telephoned Colonel Ritchie's office, reaching Kitty Hill. "I heard what happened. I'm leaving for Paris now and I'll be in the office tomorrow morning."

"I'll give Sergeant Southwood the message," Kitty said primly.

"Do you think I might speak with Miri Winter for a moment?"

"We can't tie up the colonel's phone."

"Can you tell her I'll be in tomorrow?"

"If I see her," she said grudgingly. "I have a lot of extra work to do. I have to type the letters and place all the calls the colonel is making to contact all sorts of brass, I have to dig out information about next-of-kin and make arrangements for the body to be shipped wherever they want it, I have to make sure someone gets a uniform from the lieutenant's place to bury him in, and I'm arranging a memorial service at the American church."

Seymour murmured something sympathetic

He had about three-quarters of an hour layover before the early afternoon train left Munich for Paris. It would bring him into the city past ten o'clock that night. He considered eating sausages, sauerkraut and beer for lunch at the station eaterie, but decided to wait for what, he hoped, would be a decent meal in the dining-car.

As soon as the train had pulled out of the Munich station, he went to the dining-car.

It was a long enough trip for time to think carefully over the whole situation. He had purchased a First Class ticket, and had the privacy of an otherwise unoccupied compartment. The seats were plush, if worn, and more comfortable than the plain wooden slatted seats in Second or Third. A few German-looking in worn but well-tailored dark suits were scattered in the other First Class compartments.

It hadn't taken the Germans long to get back to business, with the Americans' help, of course, but they were a hard-working and perfectionist people, and would soon be prospering. And just as well, too. If people were making money they might be less inclined to make war. A lot of mistakes had been made all round, starting with the humiliating and debilitating conditions put on the Germans at Versailles, after World War I. This time, that mistake had not been made. (Seymour was sufficiently cynical, however, to believe other mistakes had been made.)

Once in Paris, Seymour planned to try to talk first with Colonel Ritchie yet again, working around the sergeant any way he had to. Even though the colonel usually disdained speaking with enlisted men, surely the death of the lieutenant made a difference. The colonel would have to listen now. Surely the Army would not have appointed an intermediate officer yet, someone Colonel Ritchie could hide behind, who would know nothing and "need time to get up to speed".

After buttonholing the colonel, Seymour's next order of business would be to get a hold of Miri and persuade her to quit her job and get right out of town. The ideal would be for her to go to Spain, as she had planned to do much later in the year anyway. He wanted her well out of the way until the murder and his own investigations, which he was sure were tied together, were cleared up. Much as he loved her and wanted to be near her, his primary consideration was her safety.

It would have been useful if the colonel could have listened to Nate's description of his own discoveries at Garmisch, but even if Nate could make it to Paris, it would be a long shot given the colonel's fear of truth and aversion for the privates.

Once the train was out of the city and was rumbling through the countryside the signs of devastation from the war disappeared and the passing farms looked serene and timeless. Once again Seymour marvelled at the mass insanity that had overtaken a cultured accomplished people, leading them to behave in ways that had been savage, cruel, insane.

The dining-car already had other patrons when he entered, but it was not crowded and he was seated at once at a table covered with an immaculate white cloth and cloth napkin, and shining silver. This in itself was an improvement over the mess hall, even before the food was served.

After a delicious meal of sauerbraten and spaetzel, he returned to his compartment, noting again how sparsely occupied the First Class car was.

Seymour went carefully through all the facts and speculations he wanted to present to the colonel. He was assuming the colonel would hear him out, but he was going to assume, for the purposes of the presentation, that the colonel knew nothing. Because the colonel probably would only admit to knowing less than he did.

It would have been preferable, however, to say nothing to the colonel until he had more evidence; a clue to who was involved. But he didn't know if they could afford such a luxury of delay.

They crossed the border around two in the afternoon. The train came to a halt, customs officials came aboard, an officer in a neat gray uniform pulled open the sliding-door and entered his compartment, glanced at Seymour's papers and stamped them, gave him a polite salute and went on to the next compartment. He had not asked to examine any bags.

It was almost 11 p.m. when Seymour arrived at his apartment near *Notre Dame.* He was fatigued and didn't feel like seeking a meal outside. After a quick shower in the tiny tub with porcelain seat and and telephone-style hand-sprayer, he rummaged through the supply of food on hand: American canned goods and snacks from the PX. He was able to heat up a couple of cans of beans, and devour some peanut butter on Ritz crackers with a bottle of beer. He laid out a clean pair of khakis and a white tee shirt and fell into bed.

13

Seymour hoped to get to see Colonel Ritchie first thing when he arrived at the FOUSAP office the next morning. He was going to do his best to force the colonel to listen to him without the sergeant as intermediary. He just didn't trust Carr Southwood although he had no specific evidence to distrust him.

Seymour stuck his head into the colonel's office and asked if he could speak with him. It was as if the colonel's uniform was standing tall while the colonel himself had sagged inside it.

"Get lost, private!"

A moment later Kitty bustled over to Seymour, who was standing perplexed in the hallway outside the colonel's office, wondering what to do. Kitty informed him that Colonel Ritchie said Private Levin was to speak with the sergeant if he had anything to say.

Seymour had prepared a little speech for the colonel. But he was not going to be allowed to deliver it : "Colonel, I have had a theory about something illicit that is going on" – he wouldn't mention that he hadn't been able to tell the colonel because the latter didn't want to hear it – "that could be the motive for Lieutenant Morgan's murder. Garmisch has been experiencing losses for several months of heavy equipment, nothing that could be slipped into a coat-pocket! This had to be a major operation with a number of people involved. But the culprits have managed to alter accounting records so that it's not noticed that the equipment has gone missing. By the time the punch-cards and print-outs get to Paris, the local reports from Garmisch show no trace of these things. But reports from Mannheim, where the equipment makes its first stop in Europe do reflect the newly arrived equipment. At some point this information is purged from the reports here in Paris where they are sent on to Washington.

"Over a period of weeks, I told the lieutenant what I've just told you, but in more detail. Our chess-games covered the fact that we were talking business. He asked me to hold off looking into the matter further until he gave me an okay. Now here's what I think happened. The lieutenant was deter-

mined to identify the culprits and was doing inten-
sive questioning of every person who could have
been involved, starting from the top down with Vic
Logan, all the supervisors in the machine-room, the
soldiers in files, as well as Jackie Harris. And I think
he figured out who was involved and he confronted
them and was murdered."

But Levin never got to make the speech. The
colonel wouldn't talk to a private, and the private
didn't trust anyone else there to tell his theory. He
mulled over the possibility of simply waiting for the
arrival of the American Army investigators.

Seymour also wanted to talk seriously with
Miri, so he decided he might as well get that over
with. He wanted her to leave FOUSAP until the
killer was identified and in custody. He dropped in
on Charlie Nugent and asked if he could speak with
Miri in private. It was irregular, but so was murder.
Charlie was understanding. He offered permission
for Miri to take a long lunch hour, starting as soon
as she had typed one endorsement for Mr Jayes. By
the time she had finished it was eleven o'clock.
Charlie then told her she could go out with
Seymour, and not to come back until she was ready.

They slid into a banquette at the nearby cafe
where Miri sometimes had her morning coffee.
"Why did you need to see me so much you asked
Charlie to let me out early?"

"I want you out of this office, Miri. Immediately."

"What?"

"That's right. There's a killer in there. I don't want you exposed to anything."

"I haven't been here long enough to take any leave. Even if I wanted to, which I don't."

"Then just quit."

"Quit? Are you crazy? I don't have enough money saved yet to live in Spain for a year."

"So you'll live in Spain for five or six months instead of a year. That should be enough time to get bored, anyway. And when all this is settled here, I'll come and get you and we'll get married."

"Married? Where did you get that idea from?" Miri was actually quite excited at this proposal, never having had one before, although the thought of getting married terrified her. She had to admit to herself, though, that if she were going to marry anyone, which she was not, Seymour would probably be nice to be married to.

"We'll talk about that some other time. The main thing is to get you out of here."

"I'm not going to do any such thing, and furthermore, it's none of your business to tell me what to do." Miri did not like being bossed. "Just like when you buy *Eskimo Gervais* in the movies without asking me what I want."

Seymour was baffled. He didn't know what she was talking about.

"I'm going back to work now." She pushed him away when he tried to put his arm around her shoulder.

"Listen to me, Miri, it's not safe to be there. I can understand that you don't want to quit. Ask Charlie for a leave without pay. He likes you. He might agree. It won't be for that long. It would probably take him and Jayes longer to make up their minds on a replacement for you than to just let you take off for awhile. If you don't want to go to Spain yet, you can hang around Paris without coming near this place. We can see each other, you can paint, go to museums, it won't be forever. This case is going to be solved sometime. Anyway, Spain is too damned hot in July."

"When Marianne Logan tried to get a leave without pay they told her to quit and replaced her. With me."

"That was because she couldn't say how long she would be away."

Miri went back to her office feeling very depressed. Seymour was bossing her around too much.

Charlie had gone to lunch. The whole first floor seemed empty. She started to feel nervous. Suppose the killer was lurking right around? But why would he want to kill her? She didn't know anything. Still, she wished someone would show up, someone of course who was not the killer. She was sorry she had been unkind to Seymour, but he was being unreasonable and bossy.

As if in answer to a prayer, although of course she never prayed, in walked Private Dennis Bernardi, a reassuringly large solid man usually with a wide friendly smile. This time, however, he was far from smiling. He looked like he might burst into tears. "May I sit down?" He didn't wait for an answer, but pulled out her little straight-back guest chair, spun it around and straddled it. "You eating lunch in today?"

"I ate early."

"I feel very down," he sighed.

"Is it your love-life?"

"Sort of."

Everybody in FOUSAP knew that he was obsessed with Jackie Harris. Now Miri felt guilty that she had not told Dennis of Jackie Harris' proclivities. But she had thought maybe Jackie was AC/DC and would come around to him sometime.

"Want some advice?" Miri said kindly. "Find somebody else. Tell you what. Next time my roommate throws a party I'll tell her to invite you. Of course her crowd needs women more than they need more men but so what? One more extra man will make it nice for the few girls who show up. In fact,

I'll get her to invite the two singers on Fulbrights. You've all met already anyway, remember, at Judy Dantan's, back in May?"

Dennis nodded. "You're cute."

"Cute?" Miri did not like being considered cute, it was not serious enough. But Dennis was a sweetie so she let it pass. It was no wonder he was depressed. They all were, over the murder.

Dantan went down to the machine-room to speak briefly with Carolene Mayce. She was leaning over some hapless machine-operator who looked miserable, but straightened up when she saw the inspector, and even gave him a frosty smile.

"Just a quick question or two, *Madame* Mayce." She nodded graciously.

"You lent Private Bernardi your car this past weekend, isn't that correct?"

"It is. And he's going to take it this coming weekend too."

"That seems extraordinarily generous of you, *Madame.*"

"Oh, Dennis comes in handy," she said vaguely. "And he always returns the car spic and span inside and out with the gas-tank full up. And I'll be trading it in for a new model when I go Stateside next year. He even bought a really nice road map for the glove-compartment, for me to keep. 'Europa Touring' it's called. It's huge and has a fabric backing. I'm going to have it framed as a souvenir when I get home."

"Do you ever make use of it, *Madame* Mayce?"

She reddened. "I never go outside Paris."

"Did you happen to notice how many kilometers he put on the car this past weekend?"

"Surprisingly few. I don't know why he even bothered to borrow it."

Could it have been over a hundred miles?" Chartres was about one hundred fifty kilometers from Paris.

"Oh no! Nowheres near that."

Dantan thanked her and went to seek out Private Bernardi. It was time to question him at the P.J. Although he did not see a connection between the murder per se and a lie about the length of a drive, the lie, given Private Bernardi's intense anxiety about something, piled on more suspicion.

None of the other inspectors were around when the two men. arrived at the P.J., to which they had gone by taxi. A copy of a forensic report concerning the examination of the stairway, balustrades, all rooms on first and second floor was on Dantan's desk.

Everything was found to be oddly clean. No fingerprints, no shoe marks, not even any dust. And the cleaning-woman had not yet been there that week. The technicians did find minute traces of a white powder,which when subjected to chemical analysis was found to be cleansing powder. The chemist thought that it was probably an American brand.

Seemed like the killer did a thorough job of cleaning up after himself!

Private Bernardi had been squirming while Dantan read the report. He started when Dantan asked him the first question. "Private Bernardi, where did you really go in *Madame* Mayce's car last weekend? I don't think it was Chartres."

But Bernardi would not reply. He reddened, shaking his head.

"What time did you leave the office Friday evening?"

Bernardi answered promptly: "Five-thirty."

"Was anyone still there when you left?"

"I didn't see anyone, I don't know."

"And where did you go?"

Again Bernardi retreated into himself.

Without clearcut evidence and reason to do so Dantan was reluctant to push an American too far in an interrrogation. With a Frenchman he would have had a freer hand. But he was dissatisfied about how little he had learned.

They returned in a taxi together to FOUSAP in silence. Dantan had failed to achieve his intended purpose of intimidating Bernardi by bringing him to the P.J. for questioning.

Seymour was in conversation with Charlie Nugent when Dantan returned.

Charlie had been telling Seymour that since he had hardly ever taken time off, when he suddenly asked for permission to do so he got it. He had tried to be vague about where he was going, but thanks to Kitty Hill, anyone who cared to know would learn thatCharlie was going Stateside. She had helped him get his passport.

He told Seymour that he might look in on Marianne Logan while he in the States, as her mother lived not that far from his own family. This was of very minor concern to Seymour, and he signed off casually from Charlie, and said to Dantan, "I'm glad to see you. We need to talk."

Dantan suggested that they go to a nearby *café*.

"I've been walking around feeling as if a bomb was strapped to my waist," Seymour said when they had slid into a booth and ordered two beers. "I wasn't going to tell you guys anything," Seymour said, "just let the colonel sort it out with the brass who come to investigate, but he won't hear me out. So I'm going to stick my neck out and tell you. After all, it might help you solve the murder, it's not as if I'm committing treason, although if he found out, the colonel might view it that way....

" I had discovered that fraudulent reports from Garmisch were being filed in the Paris office and I was trying to learn the details of who was doing it and how they got their information into the system. Nobody above me wanted to hear a word about it, didn't want to get involved, except for Lieutenant Morgan. I was keeping the lieutenant informed during our chess games, and when I learned of his murder, I felt in my gut that the fraud and the murder were connected. I came to Paris as soon as I could, but when I tried to see the colonel, he told me to get lost. The colonel doesn't talk to privates."

Dantan was fascinated. "Now that I hear this, I'm going to ask you to do something for me. And with me." He said he was suspicious of Private Bernardi – Seymour protested vehemently at this – and intended to follow him this weekend in his own car. He wanted Seymour to accompany him.

"Not Dennis. No way."

"He could be involved in something we know nothing about, something the lieutenant had learned. If Private Bernardi is innocent of any wrongdoing, we will have had an ardously long drive for nothing, that's all!"

Reluctantly Seymour agreed to accompany him, if only to try to protect Dennis' interests. Since Dantan already knew that Dennis would be borrowing Carolene Mayce's car for the weekend, his plan was to be ready in his own car, accompanied by Seymour, to pull out right after him Friday evening.

Seymour told Miri he would not be able to see her that Saturday night, but she shrugged it off indifferently. He knew she was still mad at him for trying to persuade her to leave until the crime was solved.

14

On Thursday, members of the U.S. Army Criminal Investigation Command showed up at the FOUSAP office, and began holding interminable meetings with Colonel Ritchie and Chief Inspector Goulette. In all their discussions they were aided by the French interpreter Armand and by an interpreter accompanying the Americans. During this time nothing more on the investigation itself was accomplished; all was discussion.

The Chief Inspector was ready with English translations of all the P.J.'s forensic reports, the medical examiner's findings, and interviews by the Inspectors. The Americans however, did not want to rely on the translations by the French, and requested copies of the original reports so that their own interpreter could translate them. This was clearly going to set back the beginning of the Americans' entry in the actual investigation, which suited Dantan just fine.

On Friday, at five-thirty, Inspector Pilieu was keeping an eye on all cars departing from the back and front courtyards. He observed Jackie Harris' red truck exiting the side driveway from the back, then from the front courtyard a brief moment later, Carolene Mayce's dark blue Buick with Dennis Bernardi at the wheel. Pilieu quickly signalled Dantan and Levin, parked, with their engine idling, across the street. They immediately fell in behind the two other vehicles, following at a distance sufficient not to be seen.

"I can't believe Dennis would get involved in a crime," Seymour sighed, "certainly not a murder. He may be a big dope, but he's not a criminal. Dantan, this is a wild goose chase."

"He lied to me about where he went with Madame Mayce's car last week, and he's been nervous as a cat whenever I've talked to him. Maybe he's not directly involved, but he knows something he's not telling, and I want to learn more about it."

Germaine had packed a huge hamper of cold chicken, hard-boiled eggs, *crudités, baguettes,* grapes, chunks of cheese, and a thermos of strong coffee. Dantan had filled up the gas-tank and brought along a can of additional fuel. They were prepared for a very long drive.

The caravan, led by the red truck, followed by Carolene Mayce's dark blue Buick, and pulled up in the rear by Dantan's black Renault, drove onto the main road to Strasbourg. They found themselves staying on it for many monotonous miles.

Dantan and Levin conversed in a desultory fashion about their respective jobs, and briefly, their women. Dantan amused Seymour with an account of Miri Winter's inadvertent contributions to his solving the case at *Rue des Ecoles*. She had made several discoveries, misinterpreting all of them, but had communicated them to Judy, with whom he was having a delightful affair at the time, having met over this case.

They stopped briefly several times, to change places at the wheel or to urinate by the side of the road, and then drove faster to catch up to the other two, who were never out of sight.

It took them almost six hours to drive the 400 kilometers (280 miles) from Paris to Strasbourg where, fortunately, the red truck parked at a brasserie, and Jackie Harris was seen entering. It was now past midnight. The two men had been taking turns driving. Now one could sleep while the other drove.

Dantan, relying on his anonymous French appearance, went into the brasserie and ordered more
food to take with them. He bought a *jeton* to make a
call in the back of the *café* to Chief Inspector
Goulette. The chief inspector told him whom to call
in Germany so that any message could be relayed
to him, since Dantan would not be able to make
inter-country long-distance calls from a *café* telephone.

It was another 200 kilometers (140 miles) to Ulm.
They thought the others would be turning off from
Ulm to Munich, about a hundred twenty-five kilo-
meters away. But Jackie turned off the road to
Munich and drove in a more southerly direction.
Seymour recognized this as a route to Garmisch.

Seymour reminisced, "I visited Ulm once.
When I was first stationed in Germany, before I got
involved with the Ordnance disappearances, I managed to get in a few sightseeing trips. Like many
other G.I.'s I took my lead from the Army newspaper *Stars and Stripes,* which ran a series on cities in
Germany worth seeing. The articles read like tour-
ist guides, nothing about the war, except for indi-
rect references mentioning casually which buildings
had been partially bombed out, but plenty of effu-
sive praise for the architecture that was left or had
been rebuilt. Ulm wasn't too far from Garmisch, it
was Albert Einstein's birthplace, and had the tallest

Gothic spire in the world. So I paid it a visit. It sure was worth seeing if you like oddities.

"But the funniest thing was what the article in *Stars and Sripes* said about Albert Einstein. It still gives me a chuckle. The article said that there were no known relatives of the noted genius living in the town now. What a joke! Of course there weren't. They had probably all been incinerated by then. The article also said that ol' Albert did not keep in touch with any of the townspeople there!" Seymour chuckled. "A masterpiece of understatement, since those so-called townspeople had probably been shipping Jews off by the carload to the death camps, and would have shipped off Einstein himself except that being the genius he was he realized early enough what was going on in Germany and left in time."

Dantan smiled at this, but felt uncomfortable too, because his own countrymen had not been guiltless in the matter of deporting Jews. Their own citizens.

"Looks like they're headed for Garmisch."

"The question is," Dantan said, "is he the lovelorn swain following his beloved, or are the two of them conspiring together about something."

Seymour did not respond. The first question made out Dennis to be a fool, the second a rogue.

In a small town about twenty miles from Garmisch the red truck pulled up at a small inn and Jackie Harris was seen getting out of her truck, carrying an overnight bag. By this time it was almost two a.m. They had been driving for around eight hours. Dantan and Seymour agreed to sleep in the car, rather than risk notice by staying at the inn, the only such place around. They took turns keeping watch. relieved themselves near the car, breakfasted on hard-boiled eggs, *baguettes* and coffee, and were ready to leave by the time Jackie Harris emerged from the inn seven hours later and jumped into her truck. The two men felt refreshed and were ready to go.

This time they drove without stops until they reached Garmisch, in about forty minutes.

In Garmisch Seymour did not feel the need to be cautious about being spotted by someone he knew. He was too well-known around the base for his presence to be suspicious. Besides, he hoped to locate Nate Roth, and wanted to engage his help.

Jackie had parked at an old formerly-distinguished hotel in the town, and went in with an overnight bag. Dantan kept a lookout on her, while Seymour took a taxi to the base to seek out Nate, whom he found at work in his usual office. They spoke briefly, Seymour told him where Dantan's car was parked, and then Seymour returned to Dantan's car, just in time, as it happened, for less than ten minutes later Jackie Harris emerged. Nate had actually arrived a few minutes at the car before

Seymour did, having hitched a ride in an Army jeep.

The three men had a chance to rest and Nate kept the lookout. It wasn't until nightfall that the caravan set off again, this time with Nate as well as Seymour in Dantan's car.

Up to this point, Dennis Bernardi had done nothing they could characterize as suspicious. He was following Jackie Harris. So far that was all. He hung around her hotel, eating at a bistro across the street where from an outside table the entrance to the hotel was visible, and doing nothing but presumably keeping an eye out for her.

Dantan still thought it possible, however, that following *Mlle* Harris was just part of some plot. Dantan found it hard to believe that a young man would drive so many kilometers and sit around in *cafés* just to keep an eye on a woman who infatuated him. Particularly since *Mlle* Harris was not particularly prepossessing as a female. A skinny sharp-faced vixen is what she looked like. And he was equally incredulous that a young woman would drive so many kilometers just to buy some old furniture.

Dantan expected to be recognized by Bernardi when he went into the bistro to make a telephone-call to the office in Germany who would call the Chief Inspector Goulette with Dantan's message. He picked up some ham and cheese sandwiches for the three of them, and had the thermos refilled with fresh strong coffee. But Bernardi had not noticed him. So Dantan startled Private Bernardi by greeting him. Dantan said down abruptly and said to Dennis, "It's time to talk more frankly, my friend."

"About what?"

"For starters, about what happened last week that so upset you."

After much hesitation and false starts, Dennis said, "I know I sound like a fool. But here's what happened. I drove to Jackie's building, parking across the street, after seeing that her truck was not in the courtyard. I sat at an outdoor table and ordered a meal, so was still sitting outside when her truck did pull into her courtyard, in a rush. She ran inside, and almost immediately a dark brown Dodge pulled into her courtyard. It looked like Vic Logan's car. The driver didn't get out. I thought, 'Oh my God, she's having an affair with Logan!' A few minutes later Jackie rushed down, carrying a long bag that could have been a golf-bag or a bag for skiis. It wasn't ski season and I had no idea that she played golf, but at any rate she flung the bag into the trunk of Logan's car, and they pulled out fast. I gave up. I finished my meal, then drove Carolene's car back to her garage and went back to my place and spent a miserable weekend."

"Why couldn't you have told me that right

away? I knew you were hiding something, and it occurred to me you might have been involved in the murder."

"I wasn't," Dennis said soberly and sadly.

Things were clearing up in Dantan's mind. He remembered the lesson of Columbus, who sailing on a false premise and by erroneous maps discovered the New World.

"Look, Dennis, instead of following *Mlle* Harris from here on out *I'll* be following her in my car, and I would like you to follow *me* in your car. We'll talk later."

Jackie Harris eventually emerged from the hotel's parking, drove off, with the two other members of the caravan behind her, this time Bernardi bringing up the rear.

Whatever Jackie's business was, it was not to purchase any antiques. She had not gone to Munich at all, and in Garmish certainly had not gone to any auction houses, galleries or used-furniture places. Now, outside Garmisch and on the road toward Ulm, she made a stop in a small village. A G.I. in a jeep pulled up near her truck, jumped out and when she had opened the back of her truck, handed over to her a stack of computer reports and a box the shape of those containing data cards. She placed these inside her truck, in a large drawer in a ponderous secretaire she had most certainly brought with her to Germany, since she had purchased none since her arrival. It was clear she was heading toward Ulm, and presumably Paris. But where she would cross into France was still a question. So far Bernardi had done nothing but tail Jackie. and now they were driving northwest.

Dantan had not ceased to suspect Private Bernardi of something beyond crazily following a skinny little woman for many hundreds, close to thousands, of kilometers. In his phone call relayed to Chief Inspector Goulette he had set up a plan in outline, actually a trap, which might reveal what was going on. Part of the problem was to determine where she would choose to cross the border into France. The other part was how to inform Chief Inspector Goulette.

At a certain point it became clear Jackie was heading toward Strasbourg. Dantan took the chance of passing her, and getting to Strasbourg first, alerting Goulette's German contact to what he had in mind and asking them to call Chief Inspector Goulette at the P.J. in Paris to verify his account of things. It meant leaving Dennis in his own car to keep an eye on events, so he asked Seymour and Nate to get into Dennis's car. At least it would inhibit Dennis from anything illicit that he might have had in mind.

At the border, Jackie waved to the French customs officers. One of them waved back.

But another signalled her to stop, then stepped up to her window and politely asked to examine the contents of her truck. She hopped out from behind the wheel and unlocked the back of the truck. There was one piece of ponderous furniture within, a secretaire. She was poised to hop back into her truck but the customs officer asked her to open each drawer and compartment of the secretaire. She had no choice but to do so. Dantan had come back outside in time to see all this transpiring.

The records, reports and data cards which had been passed to her by a GI in a jeep, were found within.

The three American soldiers had been watching all this from behind Dantan's black car. They were joined by Dantan. Dantan turned to Nate Roth. "You're the only one of us *Mlle* Harris doesn't know. Please take a look at those materials and see if you can determine what they are."

Nate had looked at enough of these with Seymour to be able to verify that they had been produced in the Garmisch finance office and were destined for the Paris finance office. The contents of the secretaire were marked and signed by witnesses.

Dantan presented himself to *Mlle* Harris, requesting that she accompany him back to Paris and the P.J.

"What about my truck?" she demanded in a shrill voice.

"That's the least of your worries," Dantan said. "It will be brought back to Paris for you." He ushered her into the back seat of his car, accompanied by a French officer. Another French officer was to drive her truck back to Paris the next morning. The three American soldiers drove back to Paris in Carolene's car, spelling one another at the wheel every couple of hundred miles.

Bernardi was distraught at what he had seen. "I can't believe this," he kept moaning over and over.

"Cheer up, Dennis," Nate said. "If you hadn't been so hypnotized by Jackie, her scheme wouldn't have been discovered. You're an inadvertent hero!"

Nate and Seymour quietly congratulated each other that their long researches had succeeded. And Seymour, knowing that at one point Dantan had suspected Dennis himself, was pleased that his friend proved to be innocent of wrongdoing.

Dantan now had the puzzle of connecting the theft of Army records with the murder at the Army office. Dantan delivered *Jackie* Harris, who had sat silently throughout the long drive, to the P.J. to be locked up until morning, when he would begin interrogating her.

He got through to Chief Inspector Goulette late Sunday night, who contacted Colonel Ritchie and apprised him of developments. The colonel saw to it that the machine-room was locked up immediately. He also telephoned Craig Jayes at home, since as the senior civilian administrator he would be working on the Jackie Harris situation.

When Vic Logan, and all the employes, both French and American, who worked in the machine-room arrived on Monday morning they found that the machine-room was locked, the door presided over by the colonel himself, together with the senior civilian administrator. The colonel informed them all coolly that the equipment required a thorough cleaning and servicing and rather than have it done piecemeal, as was usual, thereby somewhat disrupting someone's work while others worked around it, he had given permission to shut down everything and let them get to work on it all at once.

Vic Logan was seething. His authority had been usurped, and he not been informed of any such cleaning, or the necessity for it. But he could not defy the colonel. His career would be finished if he did.

Mister Jayes declared a day off for all the civilians who worked in the machine-room, except its manager, Vic Logan. This was very cheerfully received and packs of workers departed quickly before the bosses changed their minds.

Dantan understood a few things by then: the murder site, whichever floor it was, had been thoroughly cleaned before the body was discovered. By someone who had used American-type cleaning powders. This together with the eyewitness repor of the housebound old lady and Bernardi at the bistro across the street, that Jackie had taken a large bag from her apartment Friday evening and dashed off with Vic Logan, led Dantan to conclude they had gone back to clean up killing Morgan.

They had cleaned up so well that the condition of the offices was suspicious: no fingerprints, no dust, nothing that would have been expected from a normal week at the office, even as far upstairs as the large conference room.

The French justice system gave more latitude than the American in interrogating, even accusing and arresting a suspect. The American principle "Innocent until proven guilty" did not apply under French law, which could just have well said "Guilty until proven innocent". By the time Dantan sat down with Jackie Harris in his office at the P.J. the French police had completed a search of her apartment, where they found a golf-bag containing a supply of American cleaning materials, furniture polish, cleaning powders, liquids, rags, mops, some of which contained traces of blood. Confronted with this evidence, and the fact that two witnessess had seen her toss such a bag into someone's car, Jackie Harris admitted that she had driven off with Vic Logan, and together they cleaned up the second-floor, where the murder had, in fact, occurred, as well as the first floor, and the marble staircase. But she denied any involvement with the murder itself. She claimed that Logan had killed the lieutenant, and because they were both involved in the report irregularities, she agreed to help him clean up.

"What provoked the attack, *Mlle* Harris? Surely you know that even if you did not participate." It seemed to him that his sarcasm passed her by. She was, understandably tense.

Lieutenant Morgan had begun to suspect who might be involved in tampering with the reports. He asked for a meeting between Jackie Harris, as the keeper of the files, and Vic Logan, the manager of the area that produced all reports. The lieutenant demanded certain reports. From the specificity of his request they understood that Morgan knew pretty well what they were up to. The meeting took place at the end of the working day Friday, in the conference room.

What was missing from this account was Jackie's full role in the events. This was considerately provided by Vic Logan, once he learned that his confederate had put all the blame for the murder on him.

The reports were spread out on the conference table, the lieutenant and Vic Logan bending over them. As the lieutenant asked tough questions. Jackie

Harris had presumably gone back to her office. But she had slipped back into the room, and slim enough to hide between the wall and the file cabinets, suddenly emerged, and with a large wrench smashed the lieutenant on the head.

When the two confederates had signed confessions they incriminated others, in Garmisch, some of whom were in the military. So it was not completely a civilian case.

15 - EPILOGUE

Victor Logan and Jacqueline Harris were taken into custody by the U.S. Army Criminal Investigation Command, along with the soldiers at Garmisch involved in the physical thefts and the Garmisch end of the data processing. It was later established that many millions of dollars worth of military equipment had disappeared into the black market, and the conspirators had profited handsomely from their involvement.

The arrests were done quietly and quickly, with barely a whisper of scandal about the Paris office. Colonel Ritchie's retirement would be secure. He had the grace to acknowledge Private Levin's part in solving part of the problem and of keeping it discreet. He wanted to help Seymour get into officers training, but Seymour didn't want to spend a day more than necessary in the Army and chose to remain a noncom. He did however accept a promotion to Technician 5th Grade. He became the colonel's right-hand man in spite of protocol. Trust had taken its place.

Charlie Nugent returned from the States in about a week. He had gone to South Carolina to visit Marianne Logan and her supposedly sick mother. Charlie had been genuinely fond of Marianne and had his reasons to be worried for her. Mrs Flynn proved to be in very good health. In the course of a few leisurely conversations over lemonade and Mrs Flynn's excellent white cake, Charlie learned that Marianne had known that her husband was up to something improper, and had wanted no part of it. So she made up the story about her mother's health to leave as promptly as possible.

In his gentle way Charlie was able to persuade Marianne to testify if she was needed. She was unhappy at the prospect but realized it was the right thing to do. And she was grateful for his offer to help her get another job with the Army, but she didn't want to transfer back to Paris.

Private Nate Roth requested and got a transfer

back to a base in the States to serve out the rest of his tour of duty. He and Liddy, the soprano, had been corresponding since she went home during the summer and now he could see her in person again. He brought her to meet his mother. Mrs Roth was unhappy because Liddy wasn't Jewish, but had to admit she was one of the nicest persons she had ever met.

Private Dennis Bernardi also transferred out, to Garmisch. Dennis was extremely unhappy in Paris. The girl he had been obsessed with turned out to be a thief, a murderer and a disciple of Sappho. He had to get away from the place that held so many dead hopes.

Jackie Harris' family asked Kitty Hill if she would help sell the Biedermeier furniture to help pay for a private attorney for Jackie. Kitty passed the word around FOUSAP that it was for sale, and even called on several antique dealers, but none were interested.

Despite all the transatlantic telephone calls and frequent airmail letters, Judy had managed to keep her parents in complete ignorance of the murder at the U.S. Army office where her friend Miri Winter worked, and where her husband had solved the murder. She hoped she could keep it that way once they arrived in Paris in late August. She had learned a lot about filial discretion in the past months, remembering her mother's hysteria back in January when she learned of a murder at the *pension* where Judy was then living.

First of all they, wanted to see their darling, and of course the darling's husband, but they also wanted to see the progress of renovations at their large apartment. Mr Kugel was concerned at the progress reports he had gotten. "In America, the job would have been finished by now, and better."

When they did hear of the murder, they weren't very interested. It was nice that their son-in-law was doing a good job, but since their little girl had never been in danger, they gave it minimal attention.

Judy wanted to bring them to see Renee's and Miri's apartment in *Le Marais*.

"What for? It's a dump," Miri told her.

"But it's a Jewish dump. There are old refugees struggling along there. My father will find that interesting."

"Why?"

"He gives money to organizations that help refugees, people like that. One of the organizations even honored him at a banquet last year, where the tickets alone were exorbitant, to say nothing of what the fund-raisers extracted from the guests besides. I attended it with my parents. The hotel ballrom was packed with prosperous-looking men in black-tie, and well-fed women in expensive sparkling gowns. The tables were on top of one another and the waiters were rude and flung the plates around, and this was in one of the top hotels in New York City. The entertainers were big-name comedians and singers who were Jewish. I enjoyed it, especially when they called my father up to the stage and made a corny speech about how generous he was and gave him a plaque. My mother kept wiping her eyes."

"Sounds thrilling," Miri said. It was probably nice to have so much money that you liked giving it away. It was a problem Miri would never have as she wouldn't be doing anything that would make her a lot of money.

"So that's why I'm bringing my parents to see your apartment, and a tour of *Le Marais*," Judy said firmly.

Miri knew when she was defeated. She took up the subject with Renee that evening. They were eating together in their apartment because Miri couldn't stand the local food, and Renee wouldn't go out of her way to a restaurant unless she were going to meet brilliant intellectual Americans there.

Renee was impressed with what she heard of Mister Kugel's philanthropy, and when the Kugels arrived in Paris, she along with Miri and Judy took them on a tour of the Jewish Quarter of *Le Marais*. Back at the girls' apartment she served them hot tea in a glass and sticky little cakes from a local bakery. Renee lost no time in telling the Kugels about her book-in-progress. Mrs Kugel was in tears because the sticky little cakes reminded her of her grandmother and her childhood in Brooklyn. Mr Kugel was entranced with the area, both its history and its potential. And he was impressed with Renee. He promised to help her get her book published and make known to the "right people."

Miri was glad for Renee, especially after the gigantic snub she had received from those "brilliant intellectual" Americans forming a new periodical, those tall skinny lookalikes with their pale faces and snooty nasal drawls. And they all had smoked those horrid long English cigarettes, holding them dangling between their long bony fingers. They had accepted Renee's wine, cheese, and hospitality, but showed only contempt for her ideas and her book. Miri, of course, since she was a painter, not a writer, was totally beneath their attention, an invisible servant bearing platesful of snacks. Except for Branford Duane Lee, her old acquaintance from the *pension*, they had ignored her completely. And Bran hadn't been that friendly either.

While Judy and her mother began making the rounds of the expensive boutiques, Mr Kugel con-

tacted the attorney who had helped him buy (in
Dantan's name, of course) the four apartments near
the Luxembourg Gardens. Now he wanted to buy
up *Le Marais*, all the crumbling houses he could get
his hands on, because he foresaw that some day this
area would be renovated – partly thanks to him! –
and prices would zoom up. He based his forecast
on the fact that there were so many beautiful his-
torical buildings, architecturally irreplacable, but in
need of serious repairs. One of these days the French
would wake up and let foreign capital in to fix them
up.

Mr Kugel was dismayed at the disrepair of the
synagogue. But when he spoke to the *shul machers*,
the synagogue big shots, about paying for extensive
repairs, he was dismayed at their lack of financial
sense. He didn't trust them to get the job done right
and said he would pay for restorations only if he
could send one of his own people over to oversee
everything. Except for the Torahs and prayer-books
and candelabra, of course; that was the rabbis' department.

Since her father was in an expansive buying
mood, and viewing tolerantly her mother's wild ex-
travagant bills from the shops, Judy thought it a propitious moment to tell her father that she wanted to
start collecting art. And needed money to do so. She
did not mention that it had been Miri's idea for her

to become a collector, nor did she go into any details on how she proposed to find good paintings, about which, of course, she knew nothing. Her father immediately wrote her a check to get her started, saying that when he got home he would set up a trust for the ownership of the art. This was for tax reasons, but Judy didn't want to hear about them. As long as the paintings hung in her own Paris apartment and she could hold salons and be written up in the society pages and be commended by the art critics for her taste, whatever that turned out to be, her father could do whatever he wanted. He would anyway.

When Mrs Kugel heard of the sizable collection of Biedermeier furniture which the Harris family wanted to sell, she impulsively said she would buy it all. She would stash it in one or two of the immense apartments her husband was buying. Her thinking was that if someone had gone to all the trouble Jackie Harris had to collect it, there must be something to Biedermeir, although she had never seen any, or even heard of it before.

The Army brass were saved a decision of whether they were obliged to ship it all back to the States as household effects, given the circumstances, and the Harris family were so relieved to get rid of it all at once that they gave Mrs Kugel a very good price, and also told her she could keep all of Jackie's notes and writings. and the old German tomes and her translations of them on the subject.

Miri was stunned at the depth and breadth of the research, given the heinous crimes Jackie had committed. But Renee pointed out that love of culture was separate from morality. Many of the Nazis had loved classical music and the Old Masters (many of which had been confiscated from Jews who were deported to death camps.) Despite their artistic sensibilities they had no compunctions about torturing and killing a staggering number of men, women, and children.

So the elder Kugels went home with a lot of plunder, present and future, of Paris, perhaps in some token measure making up for the fortunes stolen by the French from the Jews they had cheerfully deported to the German death camps during World War Two.

Renee went off to Israel to continue research for her book. Her brother tried to persuade her to move to a kibbutz, but she wanted to stay in Jerusalem, where the intellectuals were. He was in the Israeli Army, stationed in the Negev, and planned on making it his career.

Miri kept the apartment in *Le Marais*, soon spreading out her paintings throughout all the rooms. Her housing allowance from the Army was still more than enough for the rent, even without sharing. Her big splurge was the gas bill, for heating immense quantities of hot water for her incessant baths.

She never got to like the apartment or *Le Marais* as much as she had liked her room at Reid Hall and Montparnasse. But although she was working full-time, somehow she got more painting done then than she had done before. She loved being able to afford the best quality paints, the best sable brushes, and as many rolls of canvas as she could use. And she loved having the big place to herself.

Seymour thought that instead of going to Spain Miri should get a gallery on the Left Bank to give a show of her work, but she didn't like advice and wasn't taking it now. She kept working at FOUSAP, saving to go to Spain, and passing Saturday nights at Seymour's apartment. Sometimes he came to her place, to see her latest paintings, to help her stretch canvases, and to eat *coq au vin* the way Germaine had taught her to make it. Her bed was narrow and uncomfortable. For lovemaking they needed to go to Seymour's place. Sometimes they had dinner with the Dantans. The men had become good friends, trusting and respecting each other. Occasionally, all of them trooped around museums and galleries. In the galleries they were often the only visitors.

The break occurred when Seymour bought a Bohemian ring at the PX, garnets set in gold, and tried to give it to Miri as an engagement ring. She got very upset, crazy even, because she didn't want to be tied down and bossed around and maybe even have a baby, something for which she felt totally unfit, unready, and certainly unwilling. Seymour was very hurt, and threw the ring into his old valise, where it was to remain, misplaced, for several years.

The first issue of the periodical launched by the tall thin pale brilliant American intellectuals appeared at kiosks and on shelves of English-language bookstores, and was touted in English-language newspapers. It had been christened *American Writers Abroad,* and promised to be a monthly once they got going. The first issue contained short stories, the first chapter of a first novel, a political-philosophical essay by Branford Duane Lee the Third, an interview with one of the founders (the one whose father had provided the funding, but this was not mentioned in the article), and a poem. The first issue sold out, and the publication was pronounced a success.

During the ensuing months, under Miri's tutelage, Judy acquired four paintings: one she bought at a tiny gallery near *St Julien Le Pauvre*; the tiniest church in Paris,one from a drunken Swede whose grimy beery smoky studio they visited; one from Vanessa Tate at her room in Reid Hall where Miri sent Judy alone; and one salvaged from a dustbin at the *Marché aux Puces.*

Dantan moved on to other cases, ones with French perpetrators and French victims. He never learned that his sweet litle wife had once thought of leaving him.

* * *